POACH

GWEN LINDSTROM MYSTERIES BOOK 1

CONNIE L. BECKETT

*To Joe, my travel companion and driver in chief on our
trip to Dubois.*

ACKNOWLEDGMENTS

Thank you to my writing group friends. Your input is always valuable. A big thank you to Donna for making sure my commas are in their proper places and any plot holes are filled. Joe and I stayed at the Wind River KOA while I researched the Dubois area. The staff was helpful in their recommendations and we appreciated their input about area history and attractions. A heartfelt thank you to my friends and family for supporting my writing obsession.

1

———

LACEY

"Where in the hell is that girl, anyway?" Gwen Lindstrom asked Mack as she flipped over the sign in the restaurant window from closed to open.

The dark sky had just begun to lighten, but at the early hour, dawn had not yet brightened the shallow valley where Dubois, Wyoming, lay.

Mack shrugged. "Second time this week she's been late, right?" he asked Gwen through the opening cut in the wall between the restaurant's dining area and the kitchen. He was cleaning the already spotless grill, getting it ready for the breakfast crowd soon to wander in for crisp bacon, over-easy eggs, and tender pancakes. "I still think you need to drug test her. Or you could just fire her for being late. You've done that for lesser things."

"I would, but the summer tourist season has

started, and waitress pickings are thin," Gwen explained, reaching into the fridge for squeeze bottles of the hot, homemade salsa the Café was famous for.

The girl they talked about was Lacey Stevens, but she wasn't really a girl since she was in her twenties. She had wandered in a month earlier looking for work. Gwen had taken pity on Lacey. She was a skinny little thing, shorter than Gwen's five-foot-five, and looked like it had been a long time since she'd had a decent meal. Still, her appearance was clean and neat, and her long dark hair was pulled back into a tidy ponytail. And Gwen was short-handed with Michelle on maternity leave, and most likely not coming back.

Gwen had told Lacey, "I have a spot open on the morning shift. We open at 6 a.m. That means you need to be here and ready to go before 5:45. Understand?"

Lacey nodded her agreement.

Gwen went on, "Your hair's good pulled back like that and I guess the purple is okay." It looked like the bottom half of the girl's dark hair had been dipped into purple dye. On Lacey, the look worked. Plus, did she have the standing to protest hair? Gwen fingered her earlobe with its row of earrings that ran from the top of her ear to the bottom of the lobe. She wouldn't begrudge the girl the purple. "But," Gwen continued, "you'll need to cover that." She pointed to the tattooed sleeve on Lacey's left arm that ran from just above her wrist up to where it disappeared under the pushed-up sleeve of her baggy sweater.

"I have a long-sleeved shirt I can wear," Lacey had told her, and at that Gwen hired her.

For three weeks, Lacey had arrived before the designated time and ready to work. No doubt she was a hard worker, although her nervous manner and the fact that she was always fretting, moving, and fidgeting was quite a contrast from Michelle's heavy-bellied cautious way. And, Lord, how easily the girl was distracted. A truck would rumble into the lot and Lacey, in the middle of taking a customer's order, would stare out the window until the driver shut off the motor.

Just then the door opened, and Lacey rushed in.

"Sorry, sorry," she told Gwen as she zoomed past her on her way to the back room for an apron.

Before Gwen could open her mouth to say anything, Lacey was gone, the door to the back room swinging in her wake.

Mack held up two fingers, telling Gwen twice in one week.

The first time Lacey was late, she had come in with a black eye, the makeup she applied failing to hide the bruise. Gwen had reminded Lacey that she needed to get there before 5:45 but, seeing the damage, she didn't have the heart to scold her.

"I'm so sorry. I know this is the second time, but I promise it won't happen again," Lacey told Gwen after she came back, tying the black apron with *Ranchers' Café* stenciled in red above her breast.

The bruise around Lacey's eye had turned that pukey shade of yellow-green that bruises do after a few days. What caught Gwen's attention this morning was the darkness smudged under both of Lacey's eyes. Not a bruise but definitely evidence she hadn't slept much. Gwen wondered if she had been partying late or was the boyfriend who had most likely smacked her also been responsible for the sleepless night?

Their first customer pulled into the lot, headlights sweeping the inside of the restaurant.

"I'll talk to you about it later, Lacey. Right now, we have work to do."

Gwen watched Lacey's shoulders relax with the reprieve as a second customer pulled into the lot.

The restaurant's busy breakfast time fell between 6 and 9 a.m. Lacey was even more nervous and twitchy than usual as they waited on the ranch and farm workers who rose early for work first, and then the office staff and salespeople who slipped in for a bite before their workday began. Every time someone drove into the parking lot or opened the squeaky glass door, Lacey's head jerked toward the noise, a strange expression on her face. Gwen couldn't decipher the look. Gwen wondered if it was fear, dread, or anticipation.

An unsettling tingle fluttered on the back of Gwen's neck as if Lacey watched her all morning like a dog that had an accident on the carpet and knew punishment loomed.

At 10:30, with only one couple still eating and unable to stand it anymore, Gwen poured two cups of coffee and motioned Lacey to join her at an empty booth.

"You were late again this morning," Gwen told her as soon as Lacey sat. "Why was that?" She always believed the direct approach was best. Gwen didn't give them time to formulate a lie.

Lacey's hand shook as she poured sugar into her coffee. She quickly set the sugar container back down on the table and tucked her hands under her thighs.

Gwen had grabbed a couple of silverware sets rolled in napkins before she sat down. Now she unrolled one of them, took out a spoon, and laid it on the napkin beside Lacey's mug. When she looked up from the task, Gwen saw a tear had formed at the corner of Lacey's bruised eye. Surprised, Gwen took a deep breath and began again, this time in a softer voice.

"I'm not angry," Gwen went on. "It just seems like you're upset about something. It's just you and me working the early shift and if you don't show up, I'm jacked. Especially now that it's spring and we have tourists coming through. I need to know what's going on with you."

Slowly, eyes on her mug, Lacey took the spoon and stirred the sugared coffee. Gwen had never seen her so still, so nearly motionless. If Lacey were on drugs like Mack suspected she was, could she shift from fidgety to nearly frozen that fast? Gwen wasn't sure.

Still staring at her coffee, Lacey began. "Donny, that's my boyfriend, he didn't come home last night. I was up late waiting for him."

Oh, good Lord, Gwen thought. She hated the girlfriend-boyfriend drama thing. How many times had she seen it?

This Donny had probably gone off on a bender, and he was sleeping it off in his car or in the bed of some girl he had picked up at the bar. Good riddance. Donny was probably the one who smacked her. Lacey was better off...

"I know what you're thinking," Lacey said, interrupting Gwen's thoughts. "Donny, well, Donny wouldn't do that, I mean disappear like that. He was going—" Lacey clamped her lips shut. The words she almost said locked up in the vault of her mind. Lacey took a gulp of coffee and squirmed in the seat.

Gwen stayed quiet hoping Lacey would say more. She wanted to quiz Lacey further, but one of the remaining customers waved his coffee mug in their direction and Lacey jumped up to fill it.

2

MISSING

Lacey arrived promptly at 5:40 a.m. the next morning, tapping on the heavy glass door so Gwen could let her in.

Gwen thought the boyfriend problem had been resolved until she saw Lacey's face. The bruise was the same yuck yellow and green, but the dark circles under her eyes had deepened. Lacey rushed toward the back room to grab her apron before Gwen had a chance to question her.

Friday mornings were always busy at the Ranchers' Café. This one was no exception. Lacey worked with her usual ball of quick motion as she took orders, kept the customers' coffee cups filled, and grabbed breakfast plates as soon as Mack placed them on the counter under the warming lights and dinged the bell. Unlike the day before, she only occasionally startled whenever the door opened, or a diesel truck rumbled into the lot.

Finally, customer traffic slowed. Gwen massaged her tender shoulder, counting the minutes until 2 p.m. when her afternoon manager would take over. That was when Sheriff April Erickson marched through the door.

April was Gwen's sister-in-law, her late husband's younger sister. She was tall, nearly six feet, with a strong build, and fair complexion. April and Gabe Lindstrom, Gwen's late husband, were two peas in a Scandinavian gene pod, and sometimes when Gwen saw April, her heart would give a little ping of sorrow over losing Gabe at such a young age.

Most days, April wore a smile as big as her heart, but not today. She spared a moment to nod hello to Gwen, then turned her laser focus on Lacey.

As April approached her, uniformed with the holstered pistol and accouterments of law enforcement, Lacey froze like a deer hearing the first distant shot of the hunting season.

Gwen moved closer, not in the least bit ashamed to eavesdrop on their conversation.

"You're Lacey Stevens, right?" April asked.

Lacey nodded, twisting her hands together.

"And you reported your boyfriend, one Donald Myers, missing yesterday?"

Lacey nodded again. She seemed incapable of speech.

April turned and asked Gwen, "Okay if I talk to Ms. Stevens privately for a few minutes?"

"Take whatever time you need. We're not busy," Gwen responded, doing her best to hide her disappointment. *So much for eavesdropping.*

April pointed to the door and then followed Lacey outside.

Ten minutes later, Lacey came back alone and looking upset, eyes red in their dark hollows. Gwen longed to ask if the boyfriend had turned up —most likely in jail—but just then a party of six walked in. Gwen laid a gentle hand on Lacey's arm and told her to take a few minutes to compose herself and then went to wait on the new customers.

Finally, Marilyn, the evening manager, arrived along with the afternoon wait staff. One of the regular waitresses, Susie, came in earlier to help with lunch so Gwen sent Lacey home after the lunch crowd slowed. When she told her to take off, Lacey had bolted to the back room, already untying the apron. Before the door stopped swinging, she was back through it and rushing toward the restaurant door.

"I'm gonna get some bookwork done," Gwen

told Marilyn after she cashed out a couple who had lingered over lunch.

"What did April want with Lacey?" Mack asked.

Gwen entered the kitchen to pluck a food supplier's invoice off the bulletin board so she could pay the bill.

"Her boyfriend is still MIA. Seems like she made a missing person report after she left here yesterday."

"Off on a toot, I suspect," he replied.

Gwen lifted pot lids, peering in, nostrils twitching a bit. "This one smells good. I saw a lot of servings of it go out. I'm starving."

"Chicken and dumplings. Grab a bowl and help yourself," he told her. "Lacey have any clue where her guy went?"

"No. I thought maybe he was sleeping it off somewhere, but according to Lacey, that's out of character for him."

Mack snorted.

"Yeah, I thought that, too, but no doubt she's upset. Do you know Donny, her boyfriend?" Gwen asked.

"Never met him. Could be he's been in to eat, but I don't know what he looks like. How about you?"

Gwen added grated cheese to the top of the

chicken dumplings and scooped up a spoonful while she thought.

"Nope, same as you. Lacey rarely talks about her personal life, not that we have time to chat as busy as we are in the mornings. It's weird we don't know him. Dubois isn't that big, especially in late winter when the tourists are gone.

"Yum, this is really delicious," she continued as she spooned up another fat dumpling. The sauce tasted of sage and basil and whatever secret ingredients Mack used.

Mack began working as a chef while serving in the military. After twenty years of service, he'd retired. Retirement didn't last—too boring, he'd told Gwen. First, he went to work in the kitchen of a Jackson restaurant, but soon realized the upscale Jackson Hole lifestyle wasn't a good fit for his family, and he sought work in a smaller town. Mack talked to a friend, who referred him to another friend, who recommended him to Gwen.

The timing was perfect. After Gabe died from cancer, Gwen had thought about selling out. The restaurant's income had steadily increased over the years, but the work was hard with little time off.

Gabe, her loving supporter was gone, and she couldn't muster the heart to go on. After a few months of watching Mack's competent work, she asked if he'd like to buy in as a partner. He had agreed and now managed the kitchen, hired and fired the kitchen staff, and ordered supplies. He and his wife and their grown kids were not native to Wyoming, but they had easily adapted to the area.

Gwen spooned another helping of chicken and dumplings into her bowl and headed to her office to work on the books for a while.

As Gwen was leaving the restaurant, she saw April pull back into the lot. Her sister-in-law looked unusually harried. Normally Sheriff April Erickson was a tall pillar of calm, but not today.

"Hey, Gwen. That waitress, Lacey Stevens, still here?" April asked.

"I sent her home an hour or so ago. Why?"

"Hell," April said, resting her palm on the butt of her holstered gun. "You know where she went after she got off?"

"Nope. Why?" Gwen asked. "You found her boyfriend?"

"If it's him we found on their property. It's not good news."

Gwen frowned. "What do you mean?"

Just then the sheriff's cell phone rang. She checked the caller ID and then answered. "Yeah, Jack?"

April listened for a minute, then responded, "Keep her there, I'm on the way now. And don't say anything to her. I want to observe her reaction."

April turned back to Gwen and asked, "Your car parked around back?"

"Of course," Gwen said. She lifted her keys and beeped open the door locks of the Jeep that was parked around the side of the restaurant. "Why?"

"I'd like you to come with me, if you're free, of course. I'll drive you back when we're done. We found a body in the barn behind their house. Could be Myers, but we don't have a positive identification yet. That was my deputy on the phone. Lacey just arrived home. He's on scene with her, but it'd help me out if someone Lacey knows is there when I tell her. I'll tell you what we know on the way."

Gwen beeped her key fob, this time to relock her Jeep doors, and slid into the passenger seat of April's patrol vehicle.

"So, what happened?" Gwen asked April as they drove out of the parking lot.

"Couple guys out hiking said they noticed a barn window was broken and it didn't appear anyone was home. They went to check it out and—"

Gwen snorted.

"My thoughts exactly. Their story sounded like total BS. Anyway, they peeked inside the window, just to make sure everything was secured."

Gwen snorted again.

"Inside they found a man on the ground that they claimed looked dead, so they called 9-1-1."

"Who were the two guys?" Gwen asked.

"Don't know. Hung up before they gave the 9-1-1 operator their names, and no one was on scene when the patrol officer arrived."

"Anonymous caller then?" Gwen asked.

April turned and shot a grin at Gwen that reminded her of a wolf's snarl. "Not quite. The dispatcher will have the cellphone number the call was made from."

April slowed. Spotting a narrow driveway, she pulled into it. They were outside of town now, the trees and underbrush hiding the view of the house from the street.

"How did he die?" Gwen asked.

"We haven't examined the body yet. Jay is on the way."

Gwen's heart gave a pitter-patter at the mention of Jay Marker. He owned the Dubois funeral home. As funeral director, he also served as the Fremont County coroner when needed. He was lean and handsome with silvered hair. He was Gwen's friend and sometimes lover… when they had time. With their busy work schedules, getting together didn't happen often.

April glanced over at Gwen. "That big grin on

your face couldn't be because your handsome cowboy funeral director is due to arrive, is it?"

Gwen punched her sister-in-law lightly on the shoulder, but she couldn't damper the grin.

When they stopped at the end of the driveway, they found Lacey sitting hunched on the front steps of a sad little house with a vacant look on her face. A uniformed officer stood to one side, and he lifted a hand in greeting. Around the corner of the house, tucked into the trees, stood a weathered wooden barn with crime scene tape circling a wide swath in the front.

"I had to tell her, Sheriff," the officer informed April after they got out of the car. "She insisted on looking in the barn and the only way to stop her was to say a body had been found and we had to wait."

"Damn," April muttered.

Lacey hadn't acknowledged their arrival, hadn't even moved. As she got closer to her, Gwen saw Lacey had her arms wrapped tightly around herself as if trying to hold the pieces together. Gwen sat on the porch step beside her and put one arm gently around the girl. It was hard to know what to do with this one. She had seen Lacey stiffen and pull away when a customer patted her on the back or squeezed her arm. Lacey didn't pull away from Gwen's touch, but neither did she lean into her.

Under her shirt, Gwen could feel the knobs of Lacey's backbone.

"You cold?" Gwen asked. The spring air still held a chill, especially in the shade of the trees surrounding the lot.

Lacey nodded, the first sign of acknowledgment since they had arrived. Gwen took off her fleece jacket and placed it around Lacey's shoulders. The girl shivered in the retained warmth of Gwen's body heat.

April had walked over to the deputy standing watch at the entrance to the barn, and they talked quietly.

"You know what happened?" Gwen asked Lacey.

Lacey shook her head. "All they said was there is someone dead in the barn. They won't tell me who."

She lifted her head and gave Gwen a haunted look. "Donny still hasn't come home, you know. Oh, God. Oh, God."

Lacey put her head between her knees and sobbed.

"Is there anyone I can call to come be with you? Family or a friend?" Gwen asked.

Lacey shook her head. "No one."

That question answered, all Gwen could do was to pat the girl's bony back.

3

———

FOUND

Jay arrived a few minutes later, driving the Ford van he used for transporting bodies. He spotted Gwen when he got out. His eyebrows rose, and then a smile lit his face.

Gwen got up from the front step, brushed off the seat of her pants, and went to greet him.

Lacey stayed where she sat with her head bowed and arms hugging her knees. At least her sobbing had eased some. The officer tasked to keep an eye on Lacey raised a hand in greeting and pointed to the barn.

"Body's back there, Mr. Marker."

Gwen joined Jay as he opened the back door of the van and rolled out a gurney. She wanted to give him a hug, but the officer was watching, and their situation was… complicated.

She had known Jay's wife, Lauren, back when Gwen and her husband, Gabe, were good friends with the Markers. After Gabe died, that left Gwen the odd single in the quartet, and the invitations to join Jay and Lauren for dinner or a night out had dwindled.

Gwen had mourned the loss of their friendship but understood the awkwardness of a threesome with memories of Gabe still too present. She understood it better when she learned Lauren was diagnosed with early-onset Alzheimer's. They had supported each other—Gwen and Jay—and it had developed into more than a friendship. Still, Gwen worried about what the townspeople would say, even though Lauren was in a care home and hadn't recognized her husband in a long while.

"Do you know the deceased?" Jay asked Gwen, tilting his head in the direction of the barn.

"Never met him. The girl sitting on the steps is my morning waitress. She lives here, told me earlier her boyfriend didn't make it home last night."

Jay started toward the barn, the gurney bumping over the rough ground. Gwen walked beside him.

"So, they think the boyfriend is the body in the barn?" he asked.

"I'm guessing yes but who knows, maybe the

boyfriend killed somebody, stashed the body in the barn, and took off."

Jay turned to look at her. "That possible?"

"Hard to say. Lacey came to work a few days ago with a shiner—that tell you something?"

They arrived at the crime scene tape and an officer held up a hand. Gwen knew the officer. He was a regular at the restaurant.

"Sorry, Ms. Gwen," the officer apologized. "Authorized persons only beyond this point."

"No problem, Mark," she said, pulling his name out of her memory bank at the last second.

Mark lifted the tape and Jay, stooping low, pushed the gurney under it.

Gwen wished she had taken her own car and followed April. Now the sheriff was inside somewhere, and Gwen was stuck until she could catch a ride back. She went back to the front stoop to wait beside Lacey.

"You think it might be your boyfriend?" Gwen dared to ask Lacey who had stopped crying and was now texting on her phone.

"I think so," Lacey responded in a hoarse voice. "I keep texting him, but he doesn't answer."

Gwen couldn't think of anything else to say so they just waited on the steps, each in their own thoughts.

A short time later, Jay left the barn and walked

toward them. He had on latex gloves and held something in one hand.

It was a wallet, Gwen realized, as he came to stand in front of them.

"You're Lacey?" he asked in a gentle voice.

Lacey nodded, steepling her hands over her mouth as if in prayer.

Jay opened the wallet and pulled out a driver's license. "Donald Myers, he's your boyfriend?"

She nodded again, hands still covering her mouth.

Gwen noted Jay's use of the present tense. *Does that mean...?*

"Is this Donald?" he softly asked Lacey, showing her the photo on the driver's license.

She nodded, harder this time. Tears leaked from her eyes.

April joined them. She, too, had on latex gloves.

"I'm very sorry, honey," Jay told Lacey in the same gentle tone. "Donald is deceased."

"Donny, Donny, no, no," Lacey sobbed, wrapping herself up once more and rocking with each wail.

"Sorry for your loss," April added, wading into the circle of Jay, Gwen, and Lacey.

Identity confirmed, Jay turned and started back toward the barn.

"Are you sure?" Lacey cried.

April nodded. "We're sure."

"Can I get you something?" Gwen asked Lacey. "I have Kleenex in my purse. Let me go get it."

By the time Gwen got back from April's car, tissues in hand, April had Lacey standing, one firm hand under her elbow for support. Gwen handed the package of tissues to Lacey who wiped her nose and face. The makeup she had carefully applied to hide her black eye was gone and the harsh yellow-green of the bruise lay starkly on Lacey's delicate face. It didn't escape April's notice. Gwen just wanted to march into the barn and kick the now defenseless Donny for smacking his girlfriend.

"Lacey's going to ride back to the office with me," April told Gwen. "The crime scene techs should be here soon."

"I don't want to leave Donny," Lacey sobbed and tried to pull away from April.

"They're going to take good care of your Donny," April told her. "Right now, I need your help figuring out what happened and who did this." Softly she added, "That's how we can help him best now."

"Do you mind?" April asked Gwen.

"Go. I'll ride back to town with Jay," Gwen replied.

As Lacey and April made their way to the car,

April looked back over her shoulder and gave Gwen a conspiratorial wink.

Gwen waited and waited some more. She shivered in the late afternoon chill, wishing she had asked Lacey for her jacket back. Another vehicle arrived, this one containing two crime technicians. They briefly acknowledged Gwen before opening the trunk, pulling out equipment, and starting toward the barn.

The property was surrounded by trees and brush. Gwen could barely make out the narrow break of the curved gravel drive leading out to the blacktopped road. The house was isolated, a few miles outside of Dubois. She had driven the highway countless times never realizing there was a house behind the screen of trees.

Somewhere in a treetop, a crow cawed. A wire-fenced pasture ran alongside the drive and in it a buckskin horse grazed, occasionally lifting its head to watch the activity. A horse trailer was parked between the house and the barn, but the only other vehicle she could see was the older silver Toyota sedan that Lacey drove to work.

The Toyota was not powerful enough to haul a trailer, there was no hitch on it even if it could. If that was Donald Myers in the barn, then where was his vehicle?

Another question came to her. Why hadn't

Lacey thought to look inside the barn for her missing boyfriend earlier? Was it because she had killed him after he beat her? Or was it because his vehicle wasn't there so Lacey assumed he wasn't in the barn? She had worked with Gwen the last three mornings getting off at 2 p.m. That left a lot of time unaccounted for. What had she been doing in the afternoons? What time did Donny normally get home?

Gwen had seen Donald's driver's license when Jay showed it to Lacey. She didn't recognize him from the glimpse she caught of the photo. Maybe they hadn't been in town that long; nearly everyone in Fremont County passed through the doors of the Ranchers' Café at one time or another.

The buckskin raised his head and its ears pricked toward the barn. Gwen turned to watch Jay come through the door pushing the gurney, now topped by a lumpy, dark grey body bag. He stopped, said something to one of the deputies, and waited as the deputy got into Jay's van and backed it up to the yellow crime scene tape. Jay pushed the gurney a short distance to it, opened the vehicle's back door, and slid the gurney and Donny's body inside.

Gwen joined him, and together the three of them—two alive and one not—drove back down the shaded drive and out onto the road.

"What's the story?" Gwen asked.

"Gunshots, one in the back and one through the eye."

Gwen felt a chill ripple through her. "Pistol or rifle? Or was it a shotgun?"

"Not a shotgun, no pellet pattern. I'll know more when I get him back to the mortuary."

Gwen visualized Lacey's face, recalling which eye had been bruised.

"The left eye?" she asked.

Jay turned to look at her. "How did you know?" he asked.

Gwen shrugged. "Fifty-fifty guess," she said, but her thoughts focused on Lacey's swollen left eye. Was it Lacey's final statement of revenge against her abusive boyfriend or just coincidental? She shivered.

"I have a jacket in the pocket behind your seat," Jay told her.

Gwen glanced between the seats, saw Donny's bagged body, and turned quickly back around.

Jay grinned at her. "He won't complain. But here, let me grab it."

He reached behind her seat, pulled out a fleece jacket, and gave it to Gwen. She wrapped it around her, breathing in the lingering scent of Jay's aftershave.

Better.

The cafe, and Gwen's car, was between them and the funeral home. It was comfortable being in the car with Jay, the other passenger notwithstanding.

As if he read her mind, Jay said, "If you don't mind, I'll drop the body off first. I need to get it refrigerated, and then I can take you back to your car."

Much better.

4

RETRIBUTION

It would be a while before Gwen reached her car and home.

Jay backed the Ford into the large garage connected to the funeral home. Then he hit the remote, closing the garage door to keep out prying eyes. Only then did he go to the back of the van and pull out the gurney. The wheels unfolded from beneath the gurney as soon as they cleared the van's bumper.

Gwen was the caboose in the parade as Jay rolled the body through the automatic doors and down the short hall to the preparation room. The room was clean, the equipment, floors, and metal tables sanitized until they gleamed. Still, the place always made Gwen uneasy. Jay had explained that every deceased person deserved the respect afforded, and the preparation of a body was part of the life cycle. Still, it wasn't anything Gwen wanted to dwell on.

She had already told Jackie, her daughter, grown with her own family in Denver, that when she died, she wanted to be cremated. She had explained to Jackie and her husband that it would be their decision as to what to do with her ashes. "Bury me beside your dad if you want. Just don't plop me on your fireplace mantel," she had told them.

The unsettled feeling, however, didn't stop Gwen's curiosity about Lacey's Donny.

"You got a good look at him?" Gwen asked Jay pointing to the body in its zippered bag.

"Sure, why?"

"I was wondering what he looked like. I mean, after Lacey showed up with the black eye, I had an image of some big hairy brut with a beer gut."

Jay looked at her and grinned. "Not at all like that. Remind me not to plunk my money down if you have a hunch about the winning lottery numbers."

Jay stopped at a steel door that reminded Gwen of a grocer's walk-in cooler.

"Someone from the sheriff's office will be here later to observe when I examine him. They already took possession of what I found in his pocket."

"What did you find?" Gwen asked.

"The usual things—keys, billfold, coins." He paused. "And the torn corner of a plastic sandwich bag with some kind of substance in it."

"What?" Gwen asked, her curiosity piqued.

Jay shrugged. "I have no idea. You still want to see him?"

"Yes."

"He gave her an appraising look. "I can unzip the bag enough to expose his face, but I warn you, his eye looks bad."

Gwen's dad had hunted and fished when she was a kid and the whole family pitched in to process the deer, fish, and pronghorn. If she could do that, then she could look at Donny's ruined face. She nodded her consent.

Jay unzipped the body bag a few inches so she could see. "Just don't touch," he warned as if he needed to.

Donny had been good-looking in life with dark hair and a goatee like the ones popular now with a mustache and facial hair that curved like parentheses around his mouth and chin. His skin was mottled, but in life, his face had been lean and his nose strong. There was a raw hole where his left eye had been. Gwen tried to block that image from her mind. He had been wearing a plaid shirt and the first marks of a neck tattoo peeked out from under the collar.

"Damn," she exclaimed as Jay zipped him back in. "What would you say, mid-twenties for his age?"

"His license showed twenty-four," Jay told her as he opened the walk-in door to the cooler and pushed the gurney inside.

Gwen tried to remember what Lacey had written on her employment application for date of birth. Early to mid-twenties sounded right for her, too.

Jay went over to the large stainless-steel sink and started washing his hands.

"Whoever shot him must have gotten close if they hit his eye," Gwen remarked.

"Could be, or whoever it was they were a damn good shot. There was also a gunshot wound in his back between his shoulder blades."

Gwen thought about that. "So, you think someone sneaked up and plugged him in the back and when he spun around, they shot him a second time in his face?"

Jay turned off the water and pulled paper towels from the dispenser to dry his hands. "That's one possibility. I'll have a better idea tomorrow. Back or eye, likely neither wound would have been survivable."

"When was he killed?" she asked.

Jay opened the lid of the trash container with his foot and tossed in the paper towel. Now he stood facing Gwen. Even after time in a barn examining a dead body, his khaki pants still looked crisp. Jay had rolled up his sleeves before he washed his hands and her eyes wandered over his sinewy forearms with their fine body hair.

"You are the most curious person I have ever met," he teased. "Always have been."

Gwen shrugged and then tried to look offended, but failed. What he said was true.

"I just wondered. Lacey, my waitress, worked the last two days from open to around 2 p.m. That left a lot of the day." She left the rest of her concerns dangle, not wanting to put what she feared into words.

"You're thinking she may have killed her boyfriend?"

"I just don't know. She came to work a few days ago with a big shiner. You saw it. Her left eye, just like Donny. Plus, she's been more nervous than a feral cat."

Jay went to Gwen and folded her in his arms. "Too soon to worry about that yet. Now I have a question for you."

"Alright. What?" This she said into his very warm and masculine shoulder, smelling of whatever cologne or deodorant he had put on when his day began.

"You have plans for this evening?" Jay asked, his voice husky.

She didn't.

Jay kept an apartment in the second story of the funeral home. After his wife was admitted to the care home, he had sold their family house. Too big and too many memories, he had explained to Gwen. She knew exactly what he meant. After Gabe died, she and Jackie had rattled around in their house like two abandoned souls. Later, after their daughter went off to college, Gwen had sold the 2,500-square-foot house and bought a cottage with half the space. It suited her perfectly.

"A glass of wine first," Jay told her as he poured one for her after they'd climbed the stairs to his place.

They sat close together on the couch in his apartment. He nibbled Gwen's earlobe running his tongue along the edges of her earrings. Then he worked his way down her neck. Shivering with the pleasure of his touch, Gwen unbuttoned his shirt and slid a hand along his chest, feeling the beat of his heart.

Ten minutes later, after wine and a little more make-out time on the couch, she gasped.

"First, we both need a shower."

Much later, after an pleasurable hour of lovemaking and a quick dinner of toast and scrambled eggs, Jay drove Gwen through the dark streets to pick up her car where it was still parked in the restaurant lot. He had asked her to stay the night with him, but she had a lot to think about, especially after Jay told her the officers had found a baggie of what they suspected was drugs in Donny's pocket.

Getting ready for bed, Gwen wondered if the stash in Donny's pocket could've been methamphetamine. It would've fit with what she had seen in the news lately about Wind River Valley drug busts. She slipped the T-shirt she slept in over her head and crawled between the sheets. Using drugs might explain why Lacey always seemed so fidgety.

Gwen fell asleep still analyzing the shocking events of the day.

5

ERICKSON CLAN

IT SURPRISED GWEN EARLY THE NEXT MORNING when a haggard Lacey knocked on the cafe door at the usual time.

"Come in, Lacey. Let me get you a cup of coffee. I appreciate your dedication, especially under the circumstances, but, really, I already called Sarah to cover for you today."

"Are you sure?" Lacey asked, but seemed relieved.

"I'm sure. Get some sleep, take care of what you need to do, and you can come back when you're ready. Just keep me posted."

Gwen watched Lacey shuffle her way out, passing Sarah on her way in.

Tourists, as well as their breakfast regulars, kept Gwen and Sarah hopping.

One more day, Gwen thought, *one more day, and then I get a day off.* The restaurant was closed on Mondays, and that day couldn't come fast enough.

When the crowd thinned, Gwen's thoughts turned once more to Lacey, wondering how she was doing and if the girl would even want to come back to work after the funeral.

If she were Lacey, and she had killed Donny, she'd flee the area and never again stay in that isolated house outside of town. Lacey had never mentioned having relatives or close friends in Dubois, making her ties to the community even more tenuous.

"Sarah," Gwen called out when she saw the waitress wiping syrup off a table where a family with two young children had eaten. "Is your sister still looking for part-time work?"

"Becky? I'm not sure, why?"

"You heard about Lacey's boyfriend getting killed?" Gwen asked.

"Who hasn't," Sarah said, shaking her head. "It's been all over the news, and everyone was talking about it this morning."

Gwen was well aware of the rumor scuttlebutt; morning diners had plied her for details as she refilled their coffee cups.

"Have Becky call me if she's still looking for

work. I don't know for sure if Lacey will be coming back."

"Will do," Sarah answered. "You think Lacey won't be back because she killed him? That's what everyone is saying. There are all kinds of rumors going around town that they were dealing dope. I mean, I even heard they found a meth lab out in the barn behind the house."

Gwen wasn't sure about the last. Once the town gossip line got started, facts sprouted weird appendages. Still, Jay had told her a baggie of something was found in Donny's pocket, something law enforcement suspected might be drugs. Would Jay or April have told her if they discovered evidence that something illegal was being manufactured in the barn?

"Told you we should have tested the girl for dope," Mack told Gwen when he escaped from the kitchen to pour a cup of coffee.

Gwen shrugged. "Too late for that now, and who knows if the kid is going to flee the area or come back to work."

"Hey Todd, you ever come across meth cookers when you're tramping through the woods?" Mack asked a man in a khaki uniform shirt and cargo pants sitting at one of the nearby booths.

Gwen knew Todd. He was an investigator with the Wyoming Game and Fish Department. He was also a cafe regular. The man sitting across the table was his new partner, Mark.

"Came across a guy cooking meth clear out on one of those old ranch roads one time," Todd answered. "His car got stuck in the mud when he tried to turn around. What fool takes an old Mercury down a path where you need a four-wheel drive? Anyway, he was all nervous and you could smell the solvent when you stood beside the car. We called for the sheriff, and when they got there, we found he had chemicals and containers with liquid inside the trunk. Damn if we didn't have to call a decontamination team to haul away that piece of shit car. What about you, Mark?" he asked, addressing his breakfast companion.

"Found some marijuana patches here and there, but nothing like that," Mark replied.

Todd continued, "What we're mostly finding lately is evidence that poachers have been out hunting."

Mark nodded. "We'll catch them, just a matter of time."

"What are they poaching?" Gwen asked. "I thought that had slowed down."

"It did for a while," Mark told them. "Our agency arrested four guys in Montana a few months ago. They were working their way through the Rockies and up toward the western border of

Yellowstone. They had out of season game in their trailer— elk and mule deer."

Mark went on. "Just the other day, we talked to a landowner who had his eye on a buck with a set of big non-conforming antlers he planned to take when the season opened. But one night he saw lights out in the pasture and went to take a look. He found some guys dressing down a dozen deer, including the buck he had his eyes on."

"Damn, so they're in custody now?" Mack asked, his muscular arms crossed over a grease-stained apron.

"Nope. They took off. The landowner got his license tag number but turns out it had come off a stolen truck. Far as I've heard, they haven't been apprehended."

"The close call stopped the poaching?" Sarah asked, having joined them.

"For two seconds, maybe. Been picking up again," Todd told them. "Mark and I have been out patrolling since about four this morning. Nothing, but we'll get them yet."

After lunch, Gwen spent an hour in the restaurant office catching up on bookwork and preparing the bank deposit. She locked the deposit bag in the safe for Tuesday since the bank closed at noon on Saturday.

Before she knew it, Marilyn, Gwen's evening

manager, was knocking on the frame of the office door.

"The evening staff is all here if you're ready to take off," she told Gwen.

"Almost done," she replied.

April had invited Gwen over for dinner, and she was looking forward to it. April and Rod Erickson had three boys, one in high school, one in middle school, and one still in elementary. It made for a boisterous household, and Gwen was happy both for the noise and activity, and afterward for the quiet of her little cottage with its tidy garden in the back.

Before that happened, Gwen needed to call Lacey. She had pulled her employment application out of the file earlier wondering if the girl listed any relatives, but the only contact person was the now-deceased Donald Myers. She punched in Lacey's cell phone number. No one answered, so Gwen left a message asking her to call. She thought about going by Lacey's house, but she had promised April she'd be at their house by five-thirty, and she still had potato salad to make.

———

"Yum," April said to Gwen as she lifted the aluminum foil that covered the bowl of potato salad.

"When you decide to cook, you always make the best stuff."

"Mom, I'm starving," whined Phillip, joining them in the kitchen.

"You're always starving," April told her 15-year-old-son. "And stay out of the fridge—your dad's almost done with the burgers."

"I'm starving, is it ready yet?" Sven, the 13-year-old said, echoing his brother's whine as he entered the room.

"Teenage boys," snorted April. "I swear, I can load up two carts at the grocery store, and in less than two days they've munched their way through a whole fridge full. Go outside, you two, and see if your dad is about ready."

"Hi, Aunt Gwen," said the youngest, Marcus, hugging her.

Rob and April were both tall and Gwen noticed that even 8-year-old Marcus was edging his way to her shoulder.

"You, too, kiddo," April ordered her youngest son. "Go out and see how your dad's doing. And here, take a plate out for the burgers."

"Sometimes I envy you," a smiling April told Gwen. "I wanted a daughter like your Jackie and what did I end up with—three sons. It's twenty-four-seven food, stinky sports gear, wrestling in the living room, and more food."

Gwen laughed. "With girls, it's giggling, clothes, and girl drama. Oh yeah, and boyfriends."

April set out plates and silverware on the counter. "We aren't too involved in the dating scene yet, but Phillip does spend an inordinate amount of time prepping in the bathroom."

They pulled condiments out of the fridge and opened cans of baked beans.

"I tried calling Lacey this afternoon but all I'm getting is her voice mail. Do you know if she or Donny have any family around here?" Gwen told her, breaking their busy silence.

"I don't know about her, but some guy called the office today claiming to be Donald's brother."

"Asking about what happened?" Gwen probed.

April turned to Gwen, and her blue eyes narrowed. "Mostly, he wanted to know if we had Donald's truck, trailer, and barn keys, and when he could collect his brother's things."

Gwen chewed on that for a minute.

"So, he didn't ask what happened to his brother? That would be the first thing I would ask."

"Briefly, just to ask if we have any suspects, but mostly it was about the truck and stock trailer. Apparently, the brother didn't approve of Lacey. He claims Lacey got Donald into drugs."

"And brother knows this because he lives close by?" asked Gwen.

"Somewhere in Idaho, he says," April went on. "Lacey, she's still working for you, right?"

"I guess. At least until she tells me otherwise. I told her to take whatever time off she needed."

"You spot any evidence she's using drugs, like meth?"

"I never saw her taking anything, but she's fidgety like she can't stand to be still."

April looked out the window at Rob forking the meat off the grill. "Before we're overtaken by a herd of hungry males, I need to ask. You and Mack require a drug test before you hire people for the restaurant, don't you?"

"No, although we had one grill cook come in drunk a while back, and we had the city cops do a breathalyzer test. Then Mack fired him."

"Might be a good policy to implement, starting with that Lacey," April said as Sven opened the sliding glass door for his dad.

"Mack said the same thing."

"Smart partner you have there. We'll talk later," April quickly told Gwen as the hungry herd trooped in behind Rod.

6

AWOL

THE NEXT DAY, AFTER THE SUNDAY MORNING breakfast business slowed, Gwen again tried to reach Lacey. This time all she heard was a message announcing her voicemail was full.

Crap.

There was still the question of whether Lacey would be at work Tuesday. If not, she needed to find someone to help her with the morning shift.

She was worried about the kid, too. What if Lacey, overwrought with the loss of the sole person she had listed as a family on her employment app, had overdosed? Did Donald's brother dislike her so much that he would go to their house and try to take his possessions? Gwen felt certain it was Donny who had given Lacey the black eye.

Was the brother violent, too? How far would the brother go to collect what he felt he was owed?

She thought about taking her five-foot-four-inch, forty-nine-year-old, skinny self out to Lacey's house to make sure the brother wouldn't harm Lacey, but that didn't seem like the smartest of ideas. Even if Gwen wasn't attacked, she knew April would likely arrest her just for making such a foolish decision.

What to do?

Marilyn came in early, saying she needed more work hours, so Gwen was able to leave by noon. Her house was clean, and the garden was not fully awake from the winter, so she went to the workshop off the back of the garage. The first thing Gwen did was turn on the electric wall heater to warm the small space. Next, she took a seat at the old worktable found years ago at a garage sale, pulled tools and supplies from their drawers, and began to tie new fishing flies.

Her late husband, Gabe, had loved to fly fish. At first, Gwen joined him to spend time with her new husband, but she had grown to love the sport as much as Gabe had. Their daughter had enjoyed fishing, too, at least until Jackie had morphed into an alien-like pre-teen. The family—Gabe, Gwen, and Jackie—had explored rivers and streams throughout Yellowstone Park. It was a great way to relax on the weekend, and it had been therapeutic for them all after Gabe was diagnosed with cancer that would steal him from their family.

Teasing a line across the water's surface had also been her salvation after Gabe was gone. Gwen felt most connected to him at the river's edge with the sun slanting across the sky and inhaling the scent of pure fresh air. With May around the corner, it was time to get out on the water again.

Gwen lost herself in the intricate task of making the flies and checking fishing equipment. It wasn't until her stomach growled and she looked at the time did she realize it was after four in the afternoon and she had worked past lunch. She put the flies she finished into the tackle box, cleaned up, and went inside to fix a sandwich.

While she ate, Gwen tried Lacey's phone again. No one answered and the voicemail was still full. She thought again about driving out to the house and knocking on Lacey's front door, but then had a better idea.

———

"I wondered how you were doing," Jay said when he answered the phone.

Gwen hadn't talked to him since Friday. Not that they phoned each other every day, but they did text back and forth regularly. With work, family dinner at April's, and the afternoon's absorption in preparing for the summer fishing season, she hadn't reached out to him.

"I've been trying to reach Lacey, but she's not answering the phone. I'm worried. Has she talked to you about funeral plans for her boyfriend yet?"

"Not yet. I'm finished with the exam of Donald Myers' body. The sheriff's office wanted it expedited, and business was slow, so I was able to get it done Saturday afternoon. I expect they'll release the body for burial soon."

"What did you find?" Gwen asked.

"No surprise about the cause of death. Gunshot wounds. The deputies will arrange for an examination of the bullet fragments. Looks like a twenty-two, but I'm not the expert. I sent off blood and tissue to the Wyoming Bureau of Investigation. They'll analyze them for drugs and whatever else the sheriff's office needs."

"So, they won't know for a while if he was on drugs or was drunk?" Gwen asked.

"Alcohol testing will take a couple of days. Anything else, we're looking at three-to-four weeks, depending on how busy the lab is. Hold on a minute, I have a call on the other line I gotta take."

Gwen listened to hold music while Jay took the other call.

Everyone in Wyoming knew something about firearms. She didn't hunt, but she did know that although a .22 was good for shooting small game, it wouldn't be her first choice of weapons in situations where a person might encounter a rattlesnake, wolf, or bear while tramping through the outdoors. She wondered if the .22 came from a pistol or rifle. That might have offered a clue about both the intent and the shooter.

"I'm back," Jay said, coming back on the line. "Did you say you were trying to reach Lacey?"

"Yes, why?"

"Well, that was her that just called."

Gwen felt some of the worry she had been carrying slide off her shoulders. "Good, that means she must be alright. She called about plans for Donald?"

"Yeah, wanted to know when the sheriff was going to release the body."

"What did you tell her?" she asked.

"Told her I did my part and as soon as the sheriff gives the okay, we can proceed with funeral plans."

Gwen said, "I heard he had a brother. Has he contacted you yet?"

"A brother? No one's told me anything about family. I suspect the girlfriend or the sheriff's office has been in touch with them. Anyway, Lacey wants to meet with me about arrangements. I told her I was free now if it's a good time for her to come by. She said she'd be right over."

"I need to talk to her," Gwen said, dumping the remains of the sandwich in the trash. "Be there in two minutes."

Six minutes passed before Gwen pulled into the parking lot of Jay's funeral home. It would have been five, but she took time to put on earrings, run a brush through her hair, and swipe a bit of blush across her cheeks before leaving the house. Gwen was sitting in the lobby talking with Jay when Lacey arrived.

All the nervous mannerisms Lacey had previously displayed were gone. In their place was a sad lethargy. She moved toward them like she was afraid the ground might suddenly shift under her feet and swallow her. Gwen had felt the same way after Gabe died, like the earth beneath her feet could unexpectedly turn to quicksand.

Lacey's hair was unkempt, the purple ends tangled. The bruise around her eye had faded, but the dark circles had grown even darker.

Lacey raised a hand in greeting when she stopped in front of them but didn't speak.

Jay, ever the diplomat with years of dealing with people at the worst time in their lives, rose and put an arm around the shoulders of the fragile young woman. She turned into his shoulder and sobbed.

Gwen wasn't sure what to do. She rose and went to pat Lacey on the back. Jay spoke soothingly to Lacey, but Gwen couldn't catch the words. After a while, the sobs subsided.

"Sorry," Lacey told Jay, stepping back, seeing the spots on his shirt where her tears had fallen.

"Don't worry about it," he said, gently smiling at her. "Part of the process of grieving." In a more solemn tone, he told her, "If you're ready, we can go into my office and talk about what you want done for Donald. But first, Gwen here would like to talk to you for a few minutes. That okay?"

Lacey nodded and turned on her the same sad-puppy eyes that had swayed Gwen to hire her.

"Sit, please," Gwen said, pointing to a chair.

Lacey sat and folded her hands in her lap. Gwen perched in the chair beside her and placed one hand on Lacey's thin forearm.

"Again, I want to give my condolences for your loss."

Lacey nodded, eyes focused on the floor.

"You have any family or friends to help you?" Gwen went on.

Lacey shook her head.

"How about Donald? I hear he has a brother."

At this, Lacey jerked her head up to look directly at Gwen, giving her a puzzled look. "Donny doesn't have a brother."

Gwen leaned back in the chair. "I heard his brother contacted the sheriff's office."

She didn't tell Lacey that the brother's reason for contacting them was to ask how to get the victim's things. If this brother didn't like Lacey, maybe that was the reason for her denial. Except, wouldn't the brother need to have actually met Lacey to dislike her? She wished she had thought to ask April the name of the brother.

Lacey's genuine surprise convinced Gwen Lacey wasn't lying when she denied the family relationship.

"Donny didn't have a brother," Lacey repeated.

"But maybe Donny didn't tell you about—"

"He didn't have a brother!"

"Okay then," Gwen said, dropping the subject. "The thing I need to ask you, and I apologize for the timing, is if you're still planning to come back to work? I wasn't sure if you planned to stay in the area. If not, I need to find someone to help out."

"Yes, I'm coming back," Lacey said emphatically.

"I can get someone to work in your place until —" Gwen waved a hand at Jay's office and the viewing rooms beyond it— "after the funeral if you need the time." What she didn't voice was the possibility Lacey might be arrested if evidence was found implicating her.

This time the puppy-dog eyes were gone. "I'll be at work on Tuesday. That's when you open again, right?"

"Yes, Tuesday."

"I need the job," Lacey explained softly. She swiped at her eyes.

"Good, I'll see you Tuesday morning," Gwen said and moved to stand.

"Thank you," Lacey said in a soft voice.

"Welcome."

Jay had been watching the two of them from inside his office. When Gwen rose, he came out to meet them. "Ready?" he asked Lacey.

Lacey turned back to Gwen. "I don't know what to do."

"Jay can help you with any questions you have," Gwen said and turned to leave.

"Gwen?" Lacey beckoned with a plaintive tone of voice.

Gwen turned back.

"Are you going to be here after, you know?" Lacey again flicked her eyes at Jay's office and the rooms beyond.

"I'll wait for you," Gwen answered.

7

FOSTER KIDS

JAY AND LACEY WERE IN HIS OFFICE WITH THE DOOR closed for a long time. While she waited, Gwen picked through the magazines stacked on the coffee table. Current events in the news magazines were long out of date. She finally settled on a regional magazine with stories and colorful photos of Wyoming wildlife.

She was reading a recipe for white bean chili when, finally, the office door opened. Lacey looked just as thin and bedraggled as before, but now there was a determined set to her mouth.

Jay collected documents from the printer that had chugged to life as Gwen waited. He tapped the stack on the receptionist's desk to align the pages, stapled one corner, and handed the packet to Lacey.

"Here is the itemization of costs we talked about. We can take a check, credit card, or arrange for payments, whichever you prefer."

"I'll go ahead and pay cash," Lacey told him, taking the documents. "If that's alright?"

Gwen, half-listening, perked up.

What does a funeral cost now? Gabe's had cost over $5,000, and that was years ago.

On top of the medical bills from his illness, the funeral expense had stretched their savings thin. Gabe's life insurance had helped, but it had taken a couple of months before the paperwork was finished and she received the funds. Where did Lacey, who Gwen always assumed lived one paycheck away from eviction, find enough cash to pay for a funeral? Did Donald have a cache hidden somewhere? Could money have been a motive for murder, on top of the domestic abuse?

While Gwen waited for Jay and Lacey to finish, she made up excuses in her head for keeping the conversation with Lacey short: she had things to do at home, she had to meet a friend, or the true one, that she was hungry, exhausted, and just wanted to go home to a book and early bedtime.

Now, she was curious, not only about why Lacey wanted to talk with her but also the supposed cache of cash to pay for the funeral. God help it, her cat curiosity was once again butting its furry head into her brain.

Outside the funeral home, the sun hung low in the sky and the air had chilled.

"You hungry?" Gwen asked Lacey.

"A little," she replied. "Haven't had much of an appetite since, well, you know."

"There's a restaurant close by that serves a tasty French onion soup and homemade bread. That sound good?"

Lacey agreed, and she followed Gwen down the street to the restaurant.

Along with the unexplained funds, Gwen was curious about Lacey's denial that Donny had a brother. She also wondered what April had told Lacey about the investigation into Donny's murder.

And what about the rumor of a meth lab in the barn where Donny died? So many puzzles to solve.

At the restaurant, Gwen and Lacey ordered the soup. Gwen added a side salad to her order. Lacey asked for fries. After the waitress left, Gwen dipped a cat's paw into the pool of curiosities.

"Are the deputies saying anything about suspects in Donny's death?" Gwen asked.

Lacey took a drink of water, the liquid rippling in her shaky hand. She frowned at Gwen. "They asked me a lot of questions yesterday."

"The investigators?"

"Yes."

"What kind of questions?" Gwen asked.

Lacey wore a grim expression on her face. "Questions like they think I did it…killed Donny."

In the dark, right before Gwen had fallen to sleep the night before, the same thought had crept into her mind. It made sense, the black eye was evidence they had argued. Gwen remembered how jittery Lacey had been before the body was found. That, along with the drugs, and all the violence that came with it. Plus, the .22 was a small pistol like a woman might carry.

Lacey and Donny hadn't been in Dubois long. He may have made an enemy locally, but had they been in town long enough for that enemy's anger to fester enough to kill? Making, selling, and using drugs would certainly bring bad company to the mix.

"You think I did it, don't you?" Lacey hissed.

Gwen realized she'd been turning the possibility around in her mind so long that Lacey assumed Gwen considered it true. Guilty as charged.

Lacey tossed the napkin on the table and started to rise.

"Lacey, please don't leave," Gwen said, reaching for her. "I was just surprised they were accusing you, that's all."

It was a little white lie, but then she couldn't control where her thoughts wandered in the wee night hours.

Lacey sat back down. Gwen wasn't sure if Lacey accepted her answer, or if it was because the waitress was setting the steaming bowls of soup on their table, fragrant with seasoned beef stock, browned onions, and melted cheese bread.

"I'm guessing," Gwen said after the food was set and the waitress had left, "that the sheriff must have ruled you out if you haven't been arrested."

"After they got all accusatory, I told them I wasn't going to talk to them anymore without my lawyer. They let me leave after that."

Gwen had to admire the young woman. She doubted she would have the presence of mind to stop the questioning, although didn't the guilty always ask for a lawyer on television shows?

"Who do you think wanted to harm your boyfriend?"

Lacey put fingers to her lips and Gwen watched different emotions dance across her face. Finally, Lacey shrugged, picked up a French fry, and dipped it into a pool of ketchup.

"I don't know," she replied.

Gwen thought otherwise. Lacey was holding something back. Especially after she told Jay that she had cash to pay for the funeral.

She used her spoon to cut off a bite of the cheese and bread, scooped up a spoonful of the soup, and brought it to her mouth. Chewing, she thought, *might as well wade into deeper water.*

"I heard people say they found drugs on Donny." She dipped up a second spoonful of soup and let the sentence dangle in the air.

"Donny didn't use drugs. Neither do I." This Lacey said emphatically.

Gwen let the silence spool out.

Lacey broke first. "Listen, I usually don't puke out my personal history, but I know what people are saying and I don't, well, I don't want you to think we were into that shit."

Lacey tucked a strand of hair behind one ear and took a deep breath. "Donny and I met in foster care. My mom had problems. She drank—a lot. My dad, well, I never knew him. Anyway, CPS took me away after Mom and one of her boyfriends got into a big fight and the police came and saw the condition of the house. I bounced between Mom and different foster families ever since I was seven. Finally, the judge said enough and severed her rights. Haven't seen my mom since I was twelve or so.

"I met Donny when he came to live at my last foster home. We were both about ready to age out. You know, *poof*—" she snapped her fingers— "turn eighteen and you're on your own. Donny, he was like me, in and out of foster care most of his life. He is…was I mean." At the change of tense from Donny in the present to Donny in the past, Lacey pressed a napkin to her eyes.

Gwen thought she might cry, but after a minute Lacey laid the napkin back in her lap and continued.

"Donny turned eighteen before I did. He rented an apartment in Casper, and when I turned eighteen, I joined him. What I'm trying to say is that our parents were drunks and drug addicts. We hate dope, hated the way it screwed up their lives, and ours. No way either of us would get involved after that crap."

There was more to Lacey, and to Donny, than Gwen first realized. She thought Lacey was telling her the truth, but there was still the baggie in his pocket and the unexplained money. She changed the subject.

"So, you and Donny came to Dubois from…?"

"Not directly here."

"What kind of work did Donald do?" Gwen asked.

"Running cattle, farming, putting up fence, whatever work was needed."

They ate the rest of the meal in silence. It gave Gwen time to think, and Lacey needed to eat.

Lacey was hiding something about who or why

Donny was murdered. Donny could have kept secrets from Lacey. It wouldn't have been the first time one partner hid bad deeds from the person they claimed to love. *Weren't children of alcoholics and addicts prone to getting addicted? And what about the man claiming to be Donny's brother.* These questions needed answers, but they would have to keep for another day.

"Call me if you need anything, and I'll see you Tuesday morning," Gwen told Lacey after they had finished, and Gwen paid the bill.

8

———

DILUTE

TRUE TO HER PROMISE, LACEY TAPPED ON THE CAFE door early Tuesday morning at 5:40 a.m.

"Guess you were right," Mack grumbled, as Gwen went to let Lacey in.

Most days, Gwen and Mack arrived shortly after 5:00. This Tuesday, as usual, Gwen had poured two cups of coffee for them and went to sit beside Mack at the counter. He was working on the cook staff schedule for next week but stopped when Gwen slid onto a counter stool.

"So, your sister-in-law sheriff solved the murder yet?" Mack asked.

Gwen rubbed her neck, working out the kinks. "Not yet, but I had dinner with Lacey Sunday evening. She seems like such a flake sometimes, but there's more to her than I first thought."

"As in?" Mack prompted.

"She said she and Donald were foster kids, met in one of their foster homes. Did you know that after a foster child turns eighteen, they age out of the system?"

"Tough way to jump into adulthood," Mack replied, setting his cup back onto the saucer.

"Yeah, one day you have a roof over your head and food to eat. Then they sing happy eighteenth birthday to you and *boom* you're out on the street."

"I jumped from high school into the Army," Mack told her, gathering up the schedule he'd been working on. "Big jump, but at least I had a cot and three hots. I see lots of kids out early on their own. Sometimes it's too much to handle, and they get started on booze or drugs."

Gwen looked at her watch and gathered up their cups. "The more I see of Lacey, the less I think she uses drugs or anything else."

"Didn't you say they found a baggie of dope in the dead boyfriend's pocket?" Mack asked, rolling the schedule in his fist.

"April said they found something, but doesn't that sound a little too convenient?"

That wasn't the only thing too cutesy convenient, Gwen pondered as she took their dirty cups into the kitchen.

There was the call about a dead guy from

someone who hung up before identifying himself. That somebody just happened to spy a body through a window in a place where he had no business being. There was a so-called brother that Lacey denied. And Lacey was hiding something, that Gwen knew for sure. After all, where did the money come from to pay for the funeral?

The bruise was almost healed, Gwen noticed, when Lacey returned from the back room tying an apron around her waist. She still looked haunted, but there was a determined set to her jaw.

"See, told you I'd be here," Lacey told her defiantly.

Gwen liked her for that spark. Somewhere in her difficult childhood, Lacey had developed resilience.

It would be hard going for a while, but this one will be fine.

"I only doubted for a short second," Gwen replied, smiling.

The morning was busy. Besides their regulars, tourists came in eager to escape the confines of their homes now that the snow had melted. Later in the spring and summer, more visitors would arrive to visit the Tetons and Yellowstone Park. Gwen was thankful. It had been a cold lean winter and they needed the business. Anna came in at 11:00 to help with lunch. Gwen went to tell Lacey to take a break but before she could, Lacey approached her.

"Gwen, do you mind if I leave a little early today?" Lacey asked, wringing the washrag she had been wiping the tables with.

Gwen lifted an eyebrow.

"I mean, if you need me, I can stay, but I'm supposed to pick up Donny's ashes and Mr. Marker said he has a funeral this afternoon at 2:00. I don't want to, you know, interrupt the family."

Gwen looked around at the half-empty tables before responding. "If we're not busy at 1:00 you can go. I expect since we had such a big breakfast crowd, lunch may be light."

"Thank you," Lacey replied, still twisting the cloth.

As predicted, they had few lunch customers and soon Gwen told Lacey to go ahead and clock out.

"See you tomorrow," Gwen said to a distracted Lacey. Lacey did a backhanded wave as she went out the door, and Gwen suspected there would be tears later. She'd need to ask her tomorrow if there was going to be a funeral service.

Collecting an urn of ashes may have answered one question bumping around in Gwen's head. How much did Jay charge for cremation and a simple urn? Much less than Gabe's service had cost. She'd have to ask Jay about it. Not directly about the cost of Donald's funeral, Jay would never disclose details like that, but general information. Gwen could ask him that. Even better, Gwen could invite him out for dinner. It would give them a chance to catch up.

———

Wednesday began the same except that Lacey arrived to work even earlier than the prescribed 5:45 a.m.

After Lacey donned her apron, Gwen, too curious to wait any longer, asked, "Are you planning a funeral service for Donald? I hadn't heard you mention anything. I'm just asking in case you need a day off."

Gwen already knew the answer, having had dinner with Jay. Still, she wanted to see what Lacey would say.

Lacey shook her head sadly. "There was just Donny and me. He hadn't talked to his mom for ages, ever since CPS took him away. I don't even know where she lives. I never knew his dad's name. Donny just called him the sperm donor. I already talked to the foster family where we met. The mom and I stay in touch, somewhat. They said they just got a new kid. He's disabled, MS I think, so it would be hard for them to travel here for a funeral." She shrugged. "Who else is there?"

Gwen thought again about rootless children, pushed out the door, and told to find their way. It made her sad. Her folks were long gone, but she had a brother in Colorado Springs and assorted cousins. And, of course, April was family, as was her daughter, Jackie, and her family in Colorado.

"What about a burial service? You have his ashes, right?"

Looking grim, Lacey gathered up her dark hair with the purple ends into a ponytail at the back of her head and secured it with a scrunchie.

"Right now, I don't have the money for a plot to bury him in. Rent will be due soon, and it's just me now trying to make it. Donny is due his last paycheck, but they told me since we weren't married, I can't claim it. His boss said it'd have to go into his estate." Lacey gave a sharp bark of a laugh. "If I can't afford a spot to bury his urn, I for sure can't afford a lawyer to ask for his last check."

"I know I mentioned this before, but I heard Donny's brother contacted the sheriff about claiming Donald's belongings," Gwen said. "You said you were both in foster care. Could there be a brother he lost contact with?"

Lacey narrowed her eyes and said decisively, "Like I said before, Donny was an only child. If there is some half-brother out there on his dad's side, then neither one of us knew about it."

A customer came in, the bell hanging over the door announcing his arrival. A couple arrived next and then more hungry customers wandered in. Any other questions Gwen had were lost to the busy morning.

———

When Gwen got home that afternoon, she called April.

"How's it going?" April asked.

"The usual," Gwen responded. "Busy at work and then I'm in bed before nine."

"Exciting," April laughed. "Sounds a lot like my life only with more paperwork."

"Don't forget the boys," Gwen added.

"Sure, how can I forget the noise and the, 'hey, Mom, what's for dinner.' But I wouldn't have it any other way." April sighed in that happy exhausted way moms did. "How is that Lacey girl doing?"

Gwen filled her in on the last few days and then said, "My turn to ask. How's the case going?"

"Jay submitted tissue samples to our state forensic lab to check for drugs. Toxicology tests take time, so nothing is back on that yet. We recovered bullet fragments. The state lab is testing them and running the data through different databases to search for a match. No word on that yet, either."

"Are you still looking at Lacey as a possible suspect?" Gwen asked.

April paused then replied, "She's still on our radar, but I have reservations."

"I do, too," Gwen agreed. "There was just the two of them, and it seems like they cared about each other, even factoring in the black eye. Plus, it was taking both their paychecks to make ends meet. What's the motive?"

"The black eye would do it for me," quipped April. "But you're right, it seems like an overreaction, and, of course, we don't know the whole story."

"And from what I've experienced with Lacey, she's more likely to turtle into herself than lash out."

"Agreed," answered April. "But I've been surprised before."

That part of the case scrutinized without any conclusion, Gwen changed direction. "Did you finish analyzing what was inside the baggie in Donald's pocket?"

"Meth," April answered.

Gwen thought about that for a minute. Meth was common in the area, and the rumor mill still speculated on whether Donald manufactured drugs in the barn. Before she could ask the question, April continued. "The weird thing is the meth had an incredibly low potency. It had been cut, lots."

"With what?"

"Powered baby milk formula," April said with a snort.

"Formula powder? That's just, I don't know, bizarre." Gwen didn't want to examine too closely the family dynamic of cooking methamphetamine and then having a can of baby formula close at hand to dilute it with.

"Not so unusual," April continued. "It's one of several agents that we find added to meth and not the most dangerous one. I've seen everything from talc powder to fentanyl. What is unusual is the ratio. That much dilution, it wouldn't give much of a buzz."

"You think Donald discovered that, asked for his money back, and got shot?"

"That could be one scenario. Could also be someone wanted to set him up but didn't want to use too much of their drug supply to do it. I tell you, Gwen, a lot of this doesn't make sense."

"How so?"

"We did a search of his property, house and barn, but found no other drugs or paraphernalia. And, despite the rumors, we found no drug manufacturing equipment or supplies. Then there's the anonymous caller reporting a dead body. You've seen their place, back off the road and surrounded by woods. That seem like an area someone would just saunter by?"

"No. You ask the caller about it?"

"Can't find him. Phone he used was a throw-away, and we haven't been able to track who purchased it. One other thing, and you need to keep this under your hat."

"No problem, you know I never blab what you tell me in confidence," Gwen assured her.

"Well, we found a lot of old blood in the barn. Some of it looks like it had been cleaned up, but we also found some newer hidden under loose hay."

Gwen had been holding the phone between her shoulder and ear as she puttered around the kitchen preparing something to eat. At the mention of the blood, she sank onto the kitchen chair. Her stomach roiled, and she thought she might throw up. What in the hell had Lacey and Donny been up to?

"Not human," April added.

Gwen's nausea settled a bit.

"Some kind of animal. We're still testing to see what kind."

"Fresh?" Gwen asked. Wyoming was wild game country. It wasn't unusual for locals to clean deer, elk, pronghorn, and other game in their garages or barns. "It's not hunting season now. Could it be from last fall?"

"Hard to say. Could be they dressed out a deer or something late in the season. In an unheated barn, the blood would freeze and still look relatively fresh the next spring."

"Normally, hunters clean the blood and stuff away when they're done, not bury it under hay. That way it won't draw vermin and who knows what else," Gwen added.

"Yep."

There were no answers as to who killed Donald, just more questions. She and April talked a little more about more pleasant topics and then ended the call.

Gwen took her food to the living room and ate while watching television. She called Jay and they talked for a while. After that she went to bed, eyes barely able to stay open.

9

LOT LOUNGER

Thursday started the same way most mornings did: Lacey came in, customers arrived, and the scent of cooking bacon and brewed coffee filled the air. Lacey's nervous manner was on full display today. Gwen would have suspected ADHD, Attention Deficit Hyperactivity Disorder, except that she'd seen Lacey's absolute stillness when concentrating for herself. Gwen had realized fidgety was Lacey's normal state, and her true mood could be calculated in the differences from that norm.

Today her fidget level was high: carting away dirty dishes before the customer cleared the cash register, standing on one foot and then the other while waiting to take an order, refilling coffee cups, flinching whenever a vehicle crunched through the gravel lot.

"You need a break, Lacey?" Gwen asked after she watched Lacey shift from one foot to another and suspecting she might need to use the restroom.

"No, thanks. I'm fine," Lacey told her, a smile tight on her face.

Shortly before the lunch crowd started arriving, Gwen realized a pale-faced Lacey was watching a young man leaning against the fender of her car. There was nothing out of place about him. He was dressed in the blue jeans and flannel shirt, which was standard wear in Wyoming. Pulled low over his forehead was a ball cap with the logo of a local agri-businesses. He appeared relaxed, except for the proprietary way he leaned against her car.

Lacey stood so she could observe the man but far enough away from the window that he couldn't see her.

Gwen went to her and asked, "That someone you know?"

Lacey jumped, then started wiping down the already spotless table.

"Lacey?"

With an angry snap of her wrist, Lacey tossed the bar cloth toward the coffee maker that took up a good portion of the back-counter space.

She turned toward Gwen, crossed her arms over her chest, and whispered, "He's one of Donny's friends. They came by last night wanting to borrow his truck and the stock trailer."

"Did you let them?" Gwen asked.

"Hell, no. They were Donny's friends, not mine, and I don't trust them. Plus, Donny's stuff is no more mine to lend than it is for them to borrow. Now, here's one of them trying to intimidate me into letting them use the truck. Know what I think? I think if I gave him the keys, I'd never see Donny's truck or the trailer again."

Customers began arriving for lunch, the swing shift waitress came in, and Gwen considered the man who had moved to sit in a truck parked two spaces down from Lacey's car. She also thought, as she waited on customers, about the so-called brother who had gone to the sheriff's office wanting to collect Donny's possessions. When she had a free minute, she slipped into the back office to make a call.

"Sheriff Erickson," April announced when she answered.

"Hey, April, it's Gwen. Remember when you said Donny's brother came into the station asking for assistance to collect his things?"

"I remember."

"I have a guy outside the restaurant hanging around Lacey's car. She said he's one of Donald's friends. They asked to borrow his truck and trailer last night, and she's afraid they're going to just take them and disappear. You have a description of this so-called brother?"

"I didn't talk to him. Give me a minute, and I'll ask around. I'll call you back."

The lunch crowd came, ordered, ate, paid, and left.

Between waiting tables, Gwen stood in the kitchen and ate the meatloaf special.

Around noon, another pickup pulled into the lot and parked next to the man who had since gone to perch on Lacey's car hood. They talked for a few minutes, then the hood sitter slid into the passenger seat of the second truck, and they left. Thirty minutes later they were back. It appeared they were eating and drinking something, truck doors open to the spring air. All the while, they watched people move around inside the restaurant.

Seeing the men had no intention of leaving, Gwen had Lacey wait on the tables away from the windows while she took the ones closest.

Gwen could have asked Mack to have a chat with them about lounging in the parking lot, but Mack was off today. Chuck was manning the grill this morning, and although hardy and willing, he was well into his sixties and Gwen didn't want to put him in that position.

Finally, April called back. "I talked with our dispatcher on duty the day Donny's brother came in. She's off today, but I picked her up and we did a drive-by. The guys were sitting in the truck so she couldn't get a good look. Let me drop her back home, she has to take one of her kids for a doctor's appointment, and I'll come back by. Not much I can do except chase them off if they're not bothering anyone, but I can stop and ask if they're having mechanical troubles."

"I have a better idea," Gwen told her. "Lacey and I get off in a few minutes. Usually, I stay to get bookkeeping done. I think today would be a great day to do some fishing. My Jeep's parked around back. Lacey and I can slip out the back door and leave without them noticing. I can take her home, or if she wants, she can go fishing with me for a while. Later…I don't know. I'll see what she wants to do."

"Good idea. Text me a few minutes before you head out, and I'll come by to ask if they're having car problems, give you some cover. It'll be a good time for me to learn more about those two."

Gwen explained the escape plan to a relieved Lacey. When Gwen mentioned fishing, she was surprised to hear Lacey was eager to tag along.

"I know a good place to fly fish for trout off the Wind River," Gwen told her. "I have extra equipment you can use; I couldn't get my daughter interested after she got older."

"One of my foster families liked to camp and fish," she explained. "I always enjoyed being outdoors. And my foster dad taught me how to clean fish," she added and then beamed a smile at Gwen. The smile was a rarity, and it boosted Gwen's belief that life's hard knocks had given the girl resilience.

For all the plotting, the escape plan wasn't needed after all. By the time April pulled her patrol car into the lot the two men had left.

"Crap," April told them when she came in. "Their vehicle tag was muddy the first time I went by so I couldn't see it clearly from the road."

Gwen still felt cautious. She surveyed the parking lot and then they left out the back door, walking between the dumpsters and the wall of the restaurant to Gwen's Jeep. Inside, Lacey slumped down so her head was below the window. She stayed that way until they neared Gwen's house.

Forty-five minutes after they arrived at Gwen's house, they were at her favorite spot next to Wind River, stringing flies onto their fishing lines.

"Pretty out here," Lacey told Gwen as they walked down to the water.

The stand of willows beside the water sprouted new green foliage. Gwen breathed deep, the air fresh with the scent of warming earth and sage.

"My late husband found this place," Gwen told her. "Hard to reach unless you know where you're going." She flicked her line across the top of the water. Lacey followed suit, walking along the bank in the opposite direction so their lines wouldn't tangle.

For a while only the whirling swish of line and the gurgling rush of the stream as it flowed past filled the air.

"Got one," came a hoarse whisper as Lacey's pole bent toward the water.

Gwen grabbed the net and went to help land the fish.

"I'd bet near seven pounds," Gwen said as she scooped the trout into the net.

"Supper," beamed Lacey.

Gwen thought she looked so different in this happy moment, younger and sweeter.

Lacey cleaned the fish and packed it in the ice cooler Gwen had brought along. They continued fly-fishing for a while longer, but neither had any more luck. When Gwen next looked at her watch, it was almost five-thirty. A chill had crept in with the dusk; winter still had a bit of a grip on the weather.

When she found Lacey, Gwen saw she had already attached the hook onto her pole and was making her way toward the Jeep. Gwen followed.

"I brought along a thermos of hot tea. Sandwiches, too," Gwen told Lacey after they had put their gear away and climbed into the vehicle.

"Hot tea sounds great," Lacey said, her teeth chattering.

Gwen started the Jeep to warm it while Lacey poured the tea into mugs. They sat in companionable silence for a while munching sandwiches and watching the willows sway in the breeze.

"Thank you, Gwen, for this," Lacey said after a time, waving at the scenery outside their window, "and for everything else."

"Welcome, Lacey."

"I mean, well, Donny and I didn't have much luck with the way we grew up. Least, we could trust each other. Now, I don't..." Lacey took a sip of tea; her hands wrapped around the mug to absorb the warmth.

Gwen let Lacey's unfinished sentence spool out into the air. What Lacey said next took her by surprise.

"I think Donny was involved in something before he died. Something he could have been in trouble for."

Gwen, sandwich halfway to her mouth, turned to stare at Lacey.

"Drugs?" she asked.

"Not drugs, never drugs," Lacey said emphatically.

As if the time fishing, relaxing and just being outdoors had freed her, the story came pouring out.

"Holy, shit," Gwen said when Lacey finished. What she'd learned, what Lacey told her, turned everything Gwen knew on its side.

Lacey's nervousness when Donny went missing, the man claiming to be his brother, the blood in the barn, Lacey's black eye. She knew what needed to be done, but would Lacey—someone who had learned as a child that adults could not be trusted—be willing to go along?

"My sister-in-law—"

"Sheriff Erickson," Lacey interrupted.

"Yes, the sheriff. She needs to hear this. You understand, right?" Gwen asked.

"I do, for Donny."

Lacey started shivering again so she wrapped her thin arms around herself. Gwen turned the heater up to high. Outside the Jeep, shadows deepened. Soon it would be dark. Men hunting for Lacey were out there somewhere, and they were a long way from help if it was needed. Gwen put the Jeep into drive.

10

REVELATION

"That explains a lot," April said after Gwen reached her on the cellphone and briefed her on what Lacey had told her. "You think she's willing to talk with us? Where the hell is she anyway?"

"Right here beside me. We're in my Jeep. We were out at Gabe's favorite fishing spot. We're heading back into town now."

"Oh Lordy, Gwen. With those guys lurking around? Hand the phone to Lacey so I can talk to her."

Lacey talked while Gwen drove. Now that she knew what was going on, every oncoming beam of headlights blazed ominously, and she worried who hid in the dark outside the range of the light. It had been fun before, sneaking out of the restaurant without the two men holding Lacey's car hostage seeing them.

No wonder Lacey was a nervous mess, knowing what she knew now. The lights of Dubois were ahead. Gwen wanted to call Jay, but Lacey still had her phone.

Lacey took the phone away from her ear and asked Gwen. "The sheriff asked if you know where Todd McPherson lives, he's the game warden."

"Tell her I do."

A minute more of conversation between Lacey and April.

"She wants us to meet her at the ranger's house. She's calling him now."

It eased some of Gwen's tension that they wouldn't have to drive all the way through town. The turnoff to Todd's house was at the edge of town, and they were fast approaching it.

A few minutes later, Gwen turned on her directional signal, made a left turn, and drove up a blacktop road that soon changed to gravel. At last, they turned into Todd's drive.

By the time they stepped out of the vehicle, April was pulling into the long drive behind them. Good timing. After telling her story twice already, Gwen worried Lacey would balk at having to repeat it over and over.

Better yet, the first words out of Todd's mouth when he invited them inside were, "Would you like some coffee?"

By the time the group settled, and coffee was poured, they had been joined by Todd's partner, Mark Paterson. Gwen sat beside Lacey on the couch to offer support if needed, but mostly to stall Lacey from bolting toward the door. That was a real possibility, she could feel Lacey trembling beside her.

"You're doing the right thing here for both Donny and yourself," Gwen whispered to Lacey, patting her on the knee.

"I hope so," Lacey replied with a weak smile.

"Thank you for coming forward, Lacey," April began. "This is Todd McPherson and Mark Paterson. They're investigators with Wyoming Fish and Game. Just tell them what you told me."

Lacey took a deep breath and Gwen could sense her steel herself.

"Donny didn't have much work this winter, you know, with the cold and snow and everything. I helped as much as I could, but things were tight. He'd worked last summer for a couple of ranchers. He told me he'd met friends there—John, I recall, was one. I can't remember if he ever said his last name. Anyway, he went out with John and another friend a few times on jobs. Donny didn't tell me much about what he was doing, but then I was busy working at the restaurant."

Grimly, Lacey looked around at the people gathered in the room.

Encouraging nods all around answered the look.

"Sometimes he'd come home late, but I have to get up early, so I'd be asleep when he got back."

"Go on," said Todd, encouragingly.

"Donny didn't like me or anyone else going in the barn. That's why he kept it locked. He used to hang the key on the hook inside our back door. One day I had a flat on my car. Donny was gone so I just got the key and unlocked the barn looking for one of those tire irons, you know the one, shaped like a cross."

The group nodded but no one spoke. Gwen noticed they all leaned forward, making sure to catch every word of Lacey's story.

"When I opened the door and flipped on the light, I discovered a big, gutted elk hanging on a hook from one of the beams. God, I've seen game butchered before, but coming across it all of a sudden like that scared the shit out of me."

"When was that?" Todd asked.

"It was March, the end of March."

"Outside the legal season," his partner, Mark, declared. "You said one of their names was John?"

"Yes."

"Can you describe them?" Mark asked.

"I only saw John once. Neither of them ever came inside the house. He just looked like a normal ranch hand: brown hair, scruffy beard like he hadn't shaved for a few days, taller than me but most people are. Nothing different about the clothes, jeans like most everyone wears.

"How about the second guy?" Mark asked.

"That one I never saw up close, don't even know his name. Like I said, I was usually in the house or in bed when they came by."

Todd turned to Mark. "Who were the poachers you busted in Montana?"

"Jake Bryant and Robert McConnell. They were the ones heading up operations. I don't recall there being a John."

"These two might be new," Todd surmised.

"Could be," Mark added.

"Go on," Todd told Lacey. "Did you ask your boyfriend what he was doing?"

Lacey used both hands to pull the hair off her face and then kept her fingers spread tight against her temples. "Not right away. I knew he'd be mad at me for looking inside the barn, especially since he trusted me with the key hanging on a hook by the back door."

Gwen wondered if the argument had included Donald's fists. It would explain Lacey's eye. Lacey rubbed her left eye as if confirming Gwen's suspicion.

"And then?" Todd prompted.

"I was in bed one night about a month or so ago when I heard Donny come back with the trailer. A pickup was following him. I know there were two people in it because I could see the silhouette of two heads when Donny backed the trailer up to the barn door and his headlights caught the truck.

"I clicked on the back porch light and came outside to see what was going on, but Donny marched up to the house and told me to go back inside and make him a couple of cheeseburgers, so I did."

"You didn't watch out the window?" the other ranger asked.

"No. I had to use the bathroom and get dressed. Then I fried Donny's burgers and started the coffee maker. The kitchen is on the opposite side of the barn. By the time I was done, they were gone. I did ask Donny what was going on," she continued, "but he just said a couple guys needed to store some stuff in the barn for a few days, and never mind what it was. I don't know what happened to the key for the barn after that."

That answered the question Gwen had when Donny's body was discovered; why Lacey hadn't looked in the barn when Donny first went missing.

"Can I use your bathroom, please?" Lacey asked Todd.

"Down the hall, first door on the right." Todd pointed to the darkened hallway.

Todd and Mark talked quietly as they waited for Lacey to come back. April used the time to text on her phone. Gwen wished she were back home.

When Lacey came back and sat down, Mark asked her, "Did Donald get paid for helping the two men out? How about charging for storing their stuff in the barn?"

Lacey tucked her hands under her legs as her eyes bounced around the room, looking everywhere but at Mark. Gwen hoped the girl never played poker. She couldn't bluff for shit.

"Like I said before, he told me to mind my own business. I think he did get something because suddenly we had enough to cover the rent."

"Anything happen right before your boyfriend went missing?" asked April.

"Not really."

"Not really? What does that mean?" April asked.

"Donny wanted us to move away," Lacy answered. "I didn't want to. We argued."

At that Lacey glanced at Gwen.

"Why move?" asked April.

"Don't know. Said he needed to find a better job, but he was real nervous and stuff. I went to work and when I got home his truck was gone."

No one said anything for a while. Gwen wasn't sure they had learned anything useful.

"And the barn remained locked?" asked Todd.

"Yes."

Todd turned to April. "You searched it?"

"We searched the first floor around where the body was found. A pickup registered to Donald Myers was parked inside and we searched it, too. The first search warrant didn't cover the house or stock trailer parked outside. We went back to the judge the next day for a warrant to cover those."

"Was there a hayloft?" Todd asked.

April nodded. "Sure, but access was up a rickety ladder. Lighting wasn't the best up there, either. Steve, he's one of my deputies, climbed up to take a look, but all he saw were old hay bales, the rectangular kind, not like they're doing now with the round bales. To him, it appeared there had been no one up there for some time so he just came back down the ladder."

"So, there's electricity to the barn?" Gwen asked.

Lacey nodded.

April added, "We turned on an overhead fluorescent when we were searching so there was electrical power. Why?"

Gwen was thinking about the childhood summers when she visited her aunt and uncle in Nebraska. They had a big barn and her older cousins had shown her how to operate the electric hoist mounted on the wall that was used to haul hay and supplies up to the loft. They had taken turns riding in the bucket. Up and down, they had gone, one riding while the other operated the controls that would run the lift, taking it up the wall rail and into the loft.

April's mind must have followed Gwen's because she said to Todd, "I'm thinking we need to do another search of the property."

"Yep," said Todd.

"Gwen," April said, "you can go on home while we wait on the search warrant."

Turning to Lacey, April said, "Lacey, I can run you…" She stopped, frowned. "Damn. I can't legally stop you from going home, Lacey, but I think it's smarter if you stay somewhere else tonight. The two punks hanging around your car might be just bluster, but until we know who they are, better for you to be safe. Got anyone you can stay with?"

Two pairs of eyes, one the blue of a Scandinavian summer sky, and the other a deep brown, landed on Gwen.

Gwen sighed, "All right, all right. I have a spare room. Might as well bunk with me tonight."

Lacey looked relieved.

April mouthed, "Thank you."

"I have a new toothbrush you can use. Got it from the dentist last time I went but haven't opened it yet. May have some old jammies somewhere, too. Anything you need from your house?"

Lacey shook her head. "I can wear these same clothes to work."

April said, "Lacey, if Gwen can spare you for a little while tomorrow, I'd like to bring you into the office and show you some photos, see if you can identify this John guy."

"Whenever you need her," Gwen told April after Lacey nodded her consent.

With plans made, Gwen and Lacey followed April's vehicle back down the drive and out onto the highway. Gwen drove by the restaurant on their way to her house. Lacey's car was still parked in the dark lot. They both surveyed the area, but Gwen couldn't see anyone loitering nearby. Still, there was just a sliver of moon tonight and she didn't want to find out who or what lurked in the shadows, so they left the car in the lot.

At the house, Gwen pointed Lacey toward the guest bedroom and in exhausted silence, they ate bowls of warmed beef and noodles that Gwen had cooked the day before.

After they were done, Lacy used the restroom while Gwen put the fish Lacey had caught into the freezer. Then Gwen turned out the lights and went to her bedroom.

11

HOUSE GUEST

"IT'S GOOD THEY DIDN'T MESS WITH HER CAR LAST night," April told Gwen, pointing out the restaurant window at Lacey's car.

The sheriff had arrived at the cafe shortly before ten that morning, Lacey trailing after her like a dinghy behind a speedboat.

"Least not that we can see," she added, addressing Lacey. "I'll have someone from our maintenance shop come and check under the hood before you drive it, just to make sure they didn't rig an explosive device or steal some part to leave you stranded. Stay here for a couple minutes, will you, Lacey, while I talk to the boss."

Marilyn and a substitute waitress—Gwen had given Lacey the day off anticipating the sheriff would need her—were already working. Gwen told

Marilyn she'd be back in a few minutes, and she and April went down the short hall to Gwen's office.

"What did you find?" Gwen asked April after she shut the office door to give them privacy.

"Two big freezers in the loft behind a wall of bales," she began. "One was filled with wrapped bundles of meat. Todd and Mark say most likely game meat, but they can't confirm if it's elk, deer, or bear until they do lab tests. The other had the same kind of wrapped meat, but it also held a frozen deer head with an unusual set of antlers."

April yawned and rubbed reddened eyes. "It was a damn long night. You remember that old rancher, lived north toward Yellowstone? The one who got mad when a big mule deer with a set of irregular antlers he had his eye on went missing from his property?"

"I remember," Gwen replied. "Claimed poachers stole it from him. If I remember right, he found blood and a mess of guts just off the road, but the poachers were gone."

"That's the one," April confirmed. "Bet you my next kid, the one we found last night in Myers' barn is the missing buck."

Gwen's eyebrows jumped up to her forehead. "Your next kid? Something you forgot to tell me?"

"Pregnant? No. My three are enough."

"Even if it was a daughter?" Gwen teased, ignoring April's denial.

"Okay, if I could be sure it would be a daughter. Hell, you know what I'm getting at."

"I bet Rod's happy about the news," Gwen teased.

April wadded up a newspaper flyer and threw it at her sister-in-law.

"Back to what I was saying," April grumbled as Gwen ducked. "Jumbled up on a row of bales were more than a dozen sets of antlers still attached to skulls. Two moose, four elk, a dozen-plus deer, and several pronghorn skullcaps."

"Sleeved pronghorn?" asked Gwen.

Deer and elk had antlers that were shed in the winter after breeding season and were then grown anew each spring. This was different from cows. Bovine horns stayed attached until death or until they were snipped off.

Pronghorn antelope were unique. The bucks, and to a lesser extent does, had permanent horns, shaped like a blade, that grew a keratin covering. The keratin formed a forward-facing prong, indicative of the antelope's name. Annually, starting in about March, the antelopes' bladed horns began to grow their sheath of keratin. The sleeves were then shed in the fall and winter after rutting. Since the growth and shedding of the sheaths were predictable, they served as a guide as to when the animal was taken, whether in the permitted August and September hunting season, or outside of it.

"Some of both," April said.

"What are antlers and pronghorn horns bringing nowadays?" Gwen asked.

"Anywhere from twenty bucks to a couple thousand, depending on spread and points. Of course, if it includes a stuffed and mounted head, that ups the price. I'd guess one to a couple thousand, again, depending on spread and the number of branches. I expect the one in the freezer with the irregular antlers will bring the higher price. That is if they can get it to the taxidermist before it's damaged by either freezer burn or thaw," she added.

"Still, all that could have been legal, taken in season."

April harrumphed. "Possible. But not likely, not in that quantity,"

Gwen couldn't disagree with that.

"By the way, you were right about the loft lift. It was hidden under some junk, but we followed the rails and found it."

"So, you seized everything?" Gwen asked.

"Nope. The judge signed the search warrant late last night, but we held off searching until four this morning." April yawned again, as if emphasizing the early hour.

Gwen hoped she had taken time for a few hours of sleep.

"I took a couple of uniformed deputies out with me in an unmarked car. Todd came, too. Mark, the other investigator, was posted in the woods along with another one of my deputies near the road. We needed to make sure we didn't have company. We photographed and inventoried what was there. Todd collected a few bundles of meat for testing and then we boogied out of there. Oh, yeah, took a scene tech out with us. She took prints off the freezers, but it'll take a few days to run them through all the AFIS databases. Right now, we can't link Myers' murder with the unidentified friends who Lacey claimed brought out the freezers. Or with the fools who jacked with her car in the parking lot yesterday."

"So, until then, Lacey needs to stay away from her house," Gwen said. "How long do you think? I mean, what's the plan?"

"We have something in the works. Lacey may have a part in it, and I'm going to talk with her about it. I'll keep you posted when I need her."

April made to leave but before she reached to open the office door, she turned back. "I think I know the answer, but do you have surveillance cameras outside here? I'd like to take a look at the guy lurking around Lacey's car yesterday."

"Sorry, no."

"Hell. Did you happen to get a good look?" April asked. "Enough to ID them?"

"The second one stayed in the truck. The visor was down so I didn't have a clear view of him. The lot lounger I saw better since I had Lacey stay back and I worked the tables near the front windows."

"You recognize him?"

"No, never saw him before, but I'd know it if I saw him again."

Gwen gave April a description, but it was hard to describe the nuances that made this man different from all the other slim, scruffy young men living in the area wearing boots, jeans, and Western cut shirts with brimmed hats.

April gave her a rueful smile. "No scars, tattoos, anything distinctive?"

"I do remember a couple things out of the norm. His hair was dark and on the long side, past his collar. In the back, below the bottom of the cap, the hair was bushed up like maybe there was some curl to it. And I remember as he turned, the sun hit him just right and I saw a sparkle in his ear, like an earring." Subconsciously, she reached up and fingered her own earring.

"Left or right?"

Gwen thought for a second. "Right."

———

Lacey stayed with Gwen over the next two days. It was a bit too much in Gwen's opinion, working together during the day and then returning to stay the night in the same house.

Gwen, no longer accustomed to the presence of another live body in her home, finally fled to the solitude of tying flies, earbuds in her ears, and her favorite tunes playing on the iPod. Lacey had appeared once in the doorway, and catching Gwen's annoyed expression, fled.

"I made soup," Lacey announced sometime later when Gwen, rubbing eyes tired from the detail work, joined her in the kitchen.

"It smells delicious," Gwen told her. And it did.

"Thank you. I found meatballs in the freezer, and garlic, onions, and beef stock in the pantry. There's new spinach growing in the garden, and I added orzo." Lacey ladled the soup into bowls and set them on the kitchen island. "Not fancy but—"

"Satisfying," Gwen finished.

Lacey picked up her spoon and then set it back down. "Gwen? I don't want to be in your way. Tomorrow, I'll go back to my house."

Was it the foster care system that had so attuned the senses of Lacey and other abandoned children to the first sign of rejection?

"Lacey, you're not in the way. Really. It's just…I don't know…after my husband died, my quiet home made me so sad. Then one day I realized that even though I still missed Gabe, I'd grown to enjoy the solitude."

"How long did that take?" Lacey asked. "Until you got used to being alone, I mean."

"Maybe a year. Gabe died in mid-summer. I had a rough, lonely winter, and then one day I realized a new spring had arrived. I could smell the earth coming to life and heard the birds sing."

Lacey nodded.

"Now eat your soup before it gets cold."

"Yes, boss," Lacey said, giving Gwen a mock salute with her spoon.

They finished eating and Gwen rinsed the bowls and placed them in the dishwasher while Lacey put away the rest of the soup.

"You heard anything from the sheriff or Todd and Mark?" Gwen asked.

April had filled her in earlier, but Gwen wanted to hear from Lacey what they had told her. When Lacey didn't answer right away, she turned to find her with a grim set to her mouth.

"I turned off my phone," she said.

"What? Why?"

"Because I kept getting calls from John, Donny's friend."

Gwen put down the towel she had been using to wipe the counter. "I didn't know that. What does he want?"

"Their stuff. Said Donny was holding something for them. Told me if I didn't give it to them, I'd be sorry."

"Well, shit," Gwen exclaimed. "I wonder if the guy hanging around the restaurant lot the other day was this John guy. I never saw him after that, so I had hoped they had given up and left town."

Lacey shrugged.

Gwen had an idea what stuff the men were referring to, but did Lacey?

"You tell April they've been calling you?" Gwen asked.

"Like I said, I turned my phone off."

"So, Neither April nor the rangers have talked to you lately?"

Lacey pantomimed holding up a phone and pressing a button. "Phone off."

On cue, Gwen's cell phone vibrated in her pocket. When she pulled it out, the screen showed the call was coming from April.

"Hey," Gwen answered.

April replied tersely, "I've been trying to reach

Lacey, but she doesn't answer. Now her voicemail is full. She with you?"

"Right here in my kitchen."

"Put me on speakerphone and hand it to her."

Gwen did and Lacey, having guessed from Gwen's reaction that the sheriff was angry, took the phone like someone had just asked her to hold a lit stick of dynamite.

"I've called you a dozen times. Why haven't you called me back?" the dynamite exploded over the line.

"Sorry, I just, well, I was getting calls from Donny's friend, and I didn't want to talk to him."

"And why in the hell didn't you tell me that?"

"I didn't want to bother you."

"Jesus Christ Almighty. I suppose my sister-in-law standing right beside you wasn't worried either?"

"Calm down, April," Gwen said, taking the phone back.

There was silence on the line for a minute, Gwen knew April well enough to know the woman needed time to ease her anger. Gwen heard noises in the background that sounded like the rumble of boys in another room.

In a calmer voice, April said, "Take me off speaker and hand the phone to Lacey."

"Say please," Gwen replied.

"Damn. Fine. Please, put Lacey back on."

Gwen went to her home office while the deputy and Lacey talked. She normally did her bookkeeping and the restaurant's order requests after the morning shift, or when things were slow. Lately, she hadn't had time so today she had brought a folder of paperwork home. Ten minutes later, Lacey tapped on the doorjamb.

"The sheriff wants to talk with you," Lacey said, handing the phone to Gwen.

"So, here's the plan," April told Gwen, and then explained what they needed to do that night.

12

GAME PLAN

IT WAS AFTER NINE AND DARK WHEN GWEN, WITH Lacey hunkered down beside her in the passenger seat, backed her Jeep out of the garage. Gwen was already weary to the marrow of her bones. It had been a long day at work after a short night, and once again it was past her usual bedtime.

Even though there was little traffic on the roads, Gwen still checked the side streets and the rear-view mirror in case they were being followed. Lacey remained slumped in the passenger seat, a dark hoodie pulled over her head. She stayed that way until they drove into the shelter of the fenced lot behind the sheriff's office and parked.

April and another deputy, the same one Gwen had seen at the crime scene when they discovered Donald's body, led them down the hall and into the conference room. Todd and Mark were already there drinking coffee from Styrofoam cups. Todd had a legal tablet in front of him and was writing something when Gwen and Lacey entered the room.

"Here's where we are," April said after everyone arrived, greetings were made, coffee poured, and people had settled in their chairs. "We already have officers in place in the woods around your house, Lacey. They'll watch but not move until needed."

April checked her notes and continued, "First, we've had a new development. Lacey, I'm going to have you step out of the room for a minute."

Gwen rose to follow her. "You can stay, Gwen," the sheriff told her.

After Lacey pulled the door closed behind her, April explained, "I haven't found any cause to suspect Lacey was involved in Myers' murder, but I'm still unsure how much she knew about his involvement, so this is something we keep to ourselves for right now, understand?"

The group around the table nodded their assent.

April addressed Mark, "Want to update us before we go on?"

"Will do," Mark agreed. "When the search warrant was executed, Todd and I collected a dozen sample bundles from the freezers, some from each species."

Gwen raised a brow. "Species?"

"Pronghorn and deer mostly, some moose and elk. They, either the poacher or the processor, had conveniently written the species name, the cut of meat, and date processed on the butcher paper the meat was wrapped in."

"It didn't take us long to catalog and weigh it all," Todd added.

"Anyway," Mark went on, "we got to looking and discovered a tiny, triangular pencil mark beside the processing date on some of the packages."

"Something the butcher did?" a deputy asked. "Correlates to a kill or processing date?"

"That was our first thought," Mark replied. "Except the only thing in common was that the marks were only on the grounded game. Like hamburger."

"Yeah, moose and deer burgers," Todd added.

"Then we noticed the packages marked with triangles appeared irregular in shape."

"Explain," ordered April, jotting down a note.

Todd said, "Normally, when the meat is put through a grinder the output resembles the shape of the machine's outlet, like a sausage maker where the mixture comes out in a tube shape. Here, the minced game came out loaf-shaped, all smooth and regular. The packages with hand-drawn triangles didn't have that perfect, uniform look."

"So, we ran a couple of the packages through the scanner," added Mark.

The two game wardens grinned at each other.

Cheshire cats, Gwen thought.

"Give it up," April commanded, rolling her hand in a come-along gesture. "We don't have all night."

"Spoilsport," Todd said, teasingly, but without malice. "Mark, tell them what we discovered."

"Plastic and duct-taped packages hidden in the middle of the ones with triangles."

"Drugs?" a deputy asked.

"Drugs and currency," Mark explained. There were large bills, fifties and hundreds mostly, wrapped in bundles and frozen inside the meat. We tested the packages with the drug. Methamphetamine with a high purity percentage. What I'm saying is that what we found was likely directly from the manufacturer before it would be cut for street sales. After the drug and cash packages were inserted into the loaves the meat was smoothed over it, but it wasn't a perfect job. Our working theory is that they were afraid a raid was coming, and they needed to get the product and funds out of wherever they were keeping them." He leaned back in the chair in satisfaction. The chair creaked as if in agreement.

"And Myers, who we suspect helped them poach, had no criminal history, and a nice, secluded barn back in the woods," added Todd.

"With electricity to keep the freezers going," Mark continued. "That is until the victim, for whatever reason, discovered what his friends were doing and wanted in. Or maybe he threatened to go to the police unless they gave him more money."

One of the deputies gave a low whistle. "How much was there, would you guess?" he asked Mark.

Mark said, "Hard to tell. We only collected a small percentage of the packages. There were two freezers in the loft, both containing packages of ground meat, steaks, and roasts. After the meat thawed, we counted some five thousand dollars folded inside each package we confiscated. Like I said, the drugs were high potency. I'd say several ounces tucked into each package."

Todd continued the explanation. "So, over two hundred packages were cataloged, including the dozen we took. Since we didn't know the significance of the triangular marking until later. It's hard to know how many of the ones remaining in the freezers contain drugs and currency."

Mark took up the baton of conversation. "We found currency in three of the twelve random packages we confiscated and one that contained drugs. That makes one-third. Using that rough estimate then one-third of the remaining one hundred and eighty packages would have a bonus tucked inside."

Todd had been working on a calculator as his partner talked. When Mark turned to him, Todd told the group, "A total of sixty loaded meat packages by my calculation. Take an average of five thousand dollars per currency package," he punched numbers into the calculator again. "Of course, the street value of the methamphetamine will be potentially higher after it's cut and sold on the street." He thought for a minute and plugged more numbers in. "Hard to say exactly, but it would be in the range of a quarter to half-million dollars."

"Talk about frozen assets," one of the deputies commented.

Laughter rippled around the table.

"Yeah, enough that our district supervisor is on his way from Laramie to oversee the operation," Todd said.

"It's also a powerful motive for murder," added another deputy, tapping his pencil on the table. "But doesn't that seem high? I mean, even factoring in the drugs?"

That was Gwen's thought, too. Sure, there was money in poaching and illegal drugs, but that kind of cash?

"It does seem high," another deputy added.

Todd spoke, "Mark and I have seen an increase here in the valley in both poaching and methamphetamine manufacture. These guys are out in the woods, anyway, when they're stalking game. They know the terrain, who owns the land, and how often the landowner inspects his property. Easy to set up a drug lab in an old, abandoned building. Somewhere that's not often visited by the property owner. Think of it as a bad guy business model expansion—poaching and meth."

That sent the group chuckling. Gwen pondered the truth of what Todd had said. It did make a perverse sort of sense.

"We need to find these people," April told the group. "Gwen, could you tell Lacey to come back in?"

After Lacey came back and sat in her chair, April explained things to her.

"Our officers haven't been able to identify this John friend of your Donny or his buddy. They may also have been the ones sitting on your car in the restaurant lot. Regardless, we need to have a little chat with them. You said they've been trying to reach you. What I need you to do is call them on your cell phone and arrange a meeting. You willing to do that?"

"You think they murdered Donny?" she asked the sheriff with a quaver in her voice.

"We don't have enough PC yet— probable cause — to make an arrest for the murder, but like I said we need to have a little chat with them." April then explained to Lacey what they needed. "You can help or not, your choice. I just need to know."

Gwen watched Lacey waver. She suspected one part of her wanted vengeance for Donald's murder. *What was the other—worry she would be implicated? Or was it fear for her own safety?*

While everyone waited, Lacey, head down, picked at her cuticles. After a minute, she straightened and looked the sheriff straight in the eye. "Okay, I'll do it." Her gaze wavered. "As long as I don't get hurt."

"I'll make damn sure of that," April said and pushed Lacey's cellphone toward her.

Lacey pressed the power button to turn on the phone. Beside her, Gwen watched as notices of voicemails and text messages scrolled down the screen. Lacey moaned softly. Gwen patted her arm.

April attached a cord to the phone. She plugged the other end into a machine that would record both sides of the conversation. Next, she and Todd put in earbuds attached to the recorder so they could listen to both sides.

"Just find one of the voicemails from that John

guy you said keeps calling you. We'll listen to the message, and then you call him back, understand?"

Lacey nodded. She picked up the phone, scrolled, tapped, listened to a message, took a gulp from the water bottle someone had brought for her, and pushed 'call.'

Gwen heard one, two, three rings from where she sat beside Lacey until someone picked up.

13

BAIT THE HOOK

"Hey, this is Lacey. You called earlier."

Pause.

"Sorry, I lost my phone and then the battery died."

Pause.

"I understand. I never had the key. It was on Donny's keychain, but I have it now."

She glanced at April.

April nodded.

"I don't think so. The cops locked the barn up after they took away Donny's body," she stumbled a little on the word 'body,' but to Gwen it just made Lacey sound sincere. She hoped the person on the other end of the conversation thought so, too.

"I don't think so. I mean, the house feels creepy, so I've stayed away."

Pause.

"Just friends here and there."

Listening.

"It doesn't matter who." Lacey's eyes narrowed and her spine straightened. "No, and if you want your shit, I said I'd get you the key. I don't know what's in there, and I don't care. I already gave my thirty-day notice so I'm out of there the end of the month, anyway."

There was a long pause while the caller talked.

"Hell, no, I haven't said anything to the police. They're idiots."

Lacey glanced sheepishly at April when she said it. April gave her a thumbs-up.

"It will take me a few minutes to drive there from where I'm staying."

Pause.

"Like I said, I don't want any trouble. Just get your shit out and then leave me alone."

Lacey looked around at the people sitting at the conference table while she listened. Her eyes glistened and she wiped at them with the sleeve of her shirt.

"Fine, then. Forty-five minutes." Lacey straightened in her chair. "And one more thing, I'm going to tell the friend I'm staying with that if I don't get home by morning to call the cops."

Pause.

"You, too, jerk," Lacey said. She jabbed the end-call icon and slid the phone across the tabletop.

"Sorry," Lacey told April. "I hope I didn't screw things up for you, it's just that he makes me so damn mad threatening me like that."

"You did good, Lacey," April said before turning to the officers in the room. "Wire Lacey up with audio. We don't have much time. Her car's already here in a garage bay, and a camera has been installed. It's fixed so we can put an officer in the trunk with quick access through the back seat if needed.

"Bryan—" she motioned to one of the uniformed officers— "give Jackson and McAlleroy a heads up. They're already on scene. Let's go people, we only have thirty minutes."

Everyone moved fast after that. Officers took Lacey away to wire her for surveillance. Gwen wished she could help, but it looked like things were under control.

"You're going to be in the surveillance van," April informed her. "It'll be parked down the highway, and we have an undercover officer who'll pretend to be changing a tire in case they come in from the west. We already have cameras in place on the property, and I need you to watch and see if whoever arrives is the same man you saw hanging around outside the restaurant." April spun around as they were leaving and pointed a finger at Gwen's nose. "And you stay in the van, no matter what happens. I'll never get my brother's freaking ghost exorcised if something happens to you on my watch."

"Got it." Gwen had no problem staying snug inside the van. Let the pros, including Sheriff April Erickson, handle it.

———

Gwen rode in the back of the panel van. The magnetic sign on the door claimed it as a home repair company. A deputy, dressed in a long-sleeved tee and jeans, and with a few days' growth of facial hair showing, drove down the highway to within thirty yards of the turnoff to Lacey's house.

Gwen worried about putting Lacey in such a vulnerable position. So many things could go wrong with that much money involved. Did John seriously think Lacey would keep her mouth shut after they took what they wanted? Would they suspect someone had messed with the cleverly concealed freezers and their stash of game meat, drugs, and money? Gwen had watched spy shows where strands of hair or a thin strip of paper across a motel room door was used to alert the spy that someone had accessed a room. Did the officers unknowingly trigger such a trap?

Deputies were already in place in the loft and around the barn, but what if rounds started flying and Lacey was trapped between the good and the bad guys? She sent a little prayer toward heaven that the girl would have enough sense to flatten herself to the ground if things went sideways.

"Let me flip around in case we need to go in," the driver told Rebecca. His undercover partner was sitting with Gwen in the back of the van. "I'll park back from the turnout we just passed and get out like we've had a flat. I'll let you know when someone approaches."

"Got ya, Nate," she told him. She, like Gwen, was dressed in jeans and a sweater.

They parked, Nate got out, and Rebecca shut the blackout curtains separating the cab from the back of the van. The setup wasn't as fancy as Gwen had seen on cop shows, but there were three computer screens bolted onto one of the side walls. The monitors cast the only light. Other equipment rested on a wire rack and Becca and Gwen sat atop wheeled shop stools for easy maneuvering.

Becca thumbed on the police radio. "Surveillance in place. I have eyes on the barn loft." An arm came out from a mound of hay, The owner of the arm whistled and waved at the camera. "And audio."

Rebecca turned to the second monitor. That screen was split. One side glowed green. Gwen recognized the objects as images from a night vision camera. The other side held dim shapes at the same angle only without the night scope.

"View of the barn entrance is working, too," she announced.

Rebecca turned on the power to the third monitor. Gwen saw the dashboard of a car with the instrument panel lit. The camera must be mounted somewhere on the mirror or in the headliner. At the edge of the screen, she saw a sweatshirt sleeve and a hand tightly gripping the steering wheel. *Lacey*. Gwen heard soft, rhythmic sounds and realized she was hearing Lacey's nervous breathing.

"I have visual and audio on our CI," Becca said, referring to Lacey as the confidential informant.

"Good," came April's voice. She sounded out of breath.

"Where is the sheriff?" Gwen asked Rebecca.

"She's making her way through the woods from the neighbor's drive."

"It's very dark," Gwen commented.

"She has night vision goggles," the undercover officer told her. "The boss will be fine."

"I'm turning into my driveway," Lacey said shakily. "But I don't see anyone here."

"Stop behind your house and turn the car so the headlights shine back toward the barn," someone instructed. "Then sit tight. They'll come, I'm sure. All you have to do is hand off the keys and leave. Just stay in the car, understand?"

"Okay," whispered Lacey.

"Vehicle approaching," said Nate talking from outside the panel van. "Just passed us, but they're slowing. Hope it's not some Good Samaritan wanting to help me change a tire. Wait, no, they're turning in. Anyone have eyes on it yet?"

"Affirmative," someone replied. "Headlights coming down the lane."

"Heads up, everyone," announced April.

Gwen watched the monitor displaying the front of the barn. The night vision side exploded in blinding light. Becca clicked the keyboard and the other split of the screen with its natural lighting filled the entire monitor. A truck and stock trailer pulled into view, made a U-turn, then disappeared out of the camera's range. It appeared on screen again when the driver backed it up so that the trailer's end was nearest the barn door.

"They're here," whispered Lacey.

14

STRIKE

"Heads up, Lacey," someone instructed. "Remember, let them come to you for the keys."

In seconds, a figure appeared outside Lacey's window. Gwen couldn't see anything above his waist. The man motioned for Lacey to roll down the window. When he leaned down to talk to Lacey, his face came into view. Gwen recognized him as the man from outside the restaurant. She told Rebecca.

"Our eyewitness confirms the male at Lacey's car was one of the people seen outside her cafe," Rebecca told her co-officers over the walkie-talkie.

"Where the fuck are the keys?" the man asked Lacey, holding out his hand.

Click.

"Well, hell, that's Jake Bryant," a low voice said.

"Who?" asked another voice, just above a whisper.

"Jake Bryant, the damn poacher out of Montana we charged a few months ago."

"Quiet," demanded April, her whisper recognizable.

"That's a good girl," John/Jake Bryant told Lacey. "Now you just step out of the car."

Lacey said something unintelligible. They had told her to stay inside. Clearly, she wanted to. There was a rustle of movement. The sound of a key turning in the ignition.

Good, thought Gwen, *you gave them the key and now you can escape…*

Before she could finish the thought, a man's arm popped through the open window. The sound of a fist hitting flesh was followed by Lacey's yelp.

Gwen gasped. The man had smacked Lacey. They saw Lacey sprawled over the console between the car's front seats.

"I'm gonna kill that bastard," Rebecca exclaimed.

"Not 'til I'm done with him," Gwen growled.

"Hold, everyone," hissed April.

"Git out here," the man commanded Lacey, trying to open the car door. "And unlock the fucking barn."

Rebecca spoke into the radio. "Everyone, he's

making our CI get out of the car and open the barn door. Heads down in there."

A second man, the one who had stayed in the truck's driver's seat, got out, lifted a dolly out of the truck bed, and joined Lacey and Jake. Wobbling and rubbing one cheek, Lacey stumbled her way to the door. She fit the key into the padlock and with the second man's help, slid the big door to one side along its tracks. Jake shoved Lacey inside while the second man turned on the overhead lights.

Rebecca clicked the computer mouse and the view shifted so that two monitors, with different perspectives, revealed the inside of the barn. The new view, from a high-mounted camera, captured a wide-angle view of the interior.

The first man pointed to a low three-legged stool, like an old-fashioned one used to milk cows, and said something to Lacey that Gwen couldn't hear. Lacey took a couple of steps toward the stool and sat. He pulled zip ties out of his jacket pocket and tied her wrists together behind her back. Then he took a rope, wrapped the middle of it twice around her neck, and made slipknots on each side of her throat. He looped one of the ends up and around the beam that made up part of an old horse stall and tied it taunt. He did the same with the other end, tying it low to a pole on the opposite side. It left Lacey in the middle with her hands cuffed and trapped like a fly on a spider's web.

"Be a good, quiet girl, and we'll let you go when we're done," he told Lacey, trying to sound soothing. To Gwen's ears, he failed. Lacey must have thought so, too; her head and shoulders sagged.

"Sheriff," Rebecca said over the radio. "They just tied the girl up inside the barn. Should we hold or go in?"

Gwen leaned toward the monitor, watching Lacey. She rubbed sweaty palms on her jeans.

"Shit," April answered. "Markel, you have eyes on them?"

A click. Just a click.

"That's the deputy up in the loft," Rebecca explained to Gwen. "He's our best sharpshooter."

The sheriff hissed, "He makes a move to harm the girl, you shoot. Understand?"

Another *click.*

While Jake tied up Lacey, the second man went to the loft lift, clearing off the debris and tarp hiding it.

The elevator was a simple mechanism with a wide metal-mesh floor and back. He flipped a wall switch and a soft hum sounded. The man stepped onto the lift floor and picked up a controller attached to a rail. Using the controls, he sent the elevator up the wall on the two parallel rails that went from the floor to the ceiling.

A light tap on the van's back door made Gwen jump.

"That's probably the sheriff," Rebecca said. "Let her in, will you."

Ducking, Gwen walked to the back, fumbling in the dark to open the door. April stepped in. Stooping low, she made her way to the monitors and took the seat Gwen had just vacated.

"We have Johnson at the window. Wade is out of the car trunk and positioned outside the door just in case," April told Rebecca.

The officer clicked a button on the second monitor and Gwen could see Deputy Wade silhouetted in the red trailer lights just outside the half-open barn door.

"Get up here and fucking help me," the man in the loft shouted down to Jake.

"Hold on to your shorts. Send the fucking lift back down for me," he answered.

He made one last check of Lacey's restraints. Then he moved closer, grabbed Lacey's head, and pulled her face to his crotch. Lacey shook her head and tried to pull away, but he grabbed a fistful of hair, jammed her head against him, and pumped his hips.

In the van Gwen moaned, Rebecca gripped the monitor controller, and April growled, "I'm gonna shoot the son of a bitch."

"Me, too," Rebecca and Gwen said in unison, unable to look away from the screen.

"Goddamn it, Jake," the man in the loft cursed.

"Later," the man hissed to Lacey, her wire picking up his threat, and Lacey's sob.

Gwen let out her breath when the man walked away from Lacey. She worried about Lacey, but she had also worried the man would discover Lacey was wired.

"Sheriff?" a radio voice asked.

Before April could answer, or even decide whether to scrub the plan to rescue their CI, Lacey whispered in a voice so low they could barely hear her.

"I'm good, I'm good."

April took a deep breath and keyed her radio. "Wait until they're away from her, and we know for sure they're after the freezers. Then we'll grab them."

The three in the van watched as the lift came down, Jake stepped on, and it rose to the loft.

Rebecca rolled her chair to the third monitor and tapped a key. The view shifted to the camera mounted in the loft. The second man shoved the dolly under one edge of a freezer while Jake held the other side so it wouldn't tip.

Lacey struggled frantically. First, she half-lifted herself off the stool, sliding her bound hands behind her back, and down her skinny thighs.

"No, wait," Gwen whispered, although Lacey couldn't possibly hear. *Why isn't she just staying put? She'll strangle if she slipped.*

"What the hell?" April barked. She grabbed the walkie-talkie, her thumb hovering over the talk button. Her eyes shifted between the monitors, one camera in the loft and the other focused on Lacey.

In the loft, the freezer sat on the dolly; Jake wrapped a tie-down around both to snug it tight.

The three women in the van watched, frozen, as the action played out. Gwen clamped her hands over her mouth. Rebecca sat forward. April's finger was still poised above the talk button, her eyes on the monitors as she inched toward the van's back door. No one said a word. The only sound was Lacey's ragged breathing.

Hopping a bit to keep from stumbling, Lacy managed to pull one foot forward through the circle of her arms. Now she straddled her bound wrists, one leg in front and the other behind. Stooped over, rope tight against both sides of her neck, she tried to pull the other foot through. She bobbled, the rope tightening and loosening as she weaved left, then right. She set the foot back down and regained her balance.

Again, Lacey lifted her back foot ready to pull it through the circle of her arms. She wobbled, her heel caught. She stood awkwardly on only one leg. She hopped, trying to keep her balance, gave up the effort, and tried to sit back down on the stool.

Gwen gasped.

"Oh, shit," Rebecca muttered.

Lacey managed to get one hip on the edge of the three-legged stool before it tipped and slipped out from under her. The rope tightened and Lacey dangled, choking as her butt landed on the floor. Her head and upper torso were held up and taut.

Gwen heard gagging noises as Lacey tried to regain her footing while at the same time working to get her second foot through the circle of her arms. Except for the gagging, Lacey hadn't made a sound.

"Fuck!" April shouted. She pressed the button on the mic. "Wade, go. Lacey's going to strangle if we don't get her out of there. Johnson, cover Wade when he goes in. Markel, move."

Gwen's gaze shifted from Lacey's struggle to the other monitor. Hay exploded and out came Markel, rifle aimed at the two men just beginning to roll the first freezer toward the lift.

"Freeze, sheriff's office," Markel shouted.

"What the…" barked Jake and ducked behind the freezer. He shoved it toward Markel and bolted toward the lift.

Gwen shifted her attention back to the first monitor. Lacey had managed to pull her second foot through and struggled to stand. Her still-bound hands frantically pulled at the tightening noose around her neck.

Gwen flinched as Johnson and Wade charged through the door. Johnson aimed his shotgun at Jake who was fumbling with the lift controller.

"Freeze. right there".

Jake wisely dropped the controller and raised his hands.

On the monitor, Gwen watched April race toward the barn.

Wade rushed to help Lacey, her face turning crimson. In one motion, he lifted her to release the pressure and pulled a folding knife out of his pocket. Swiftly, he sawed the rope until one side broke free. The pressure around Lacey's neck released. She gasped for air.

On the loft monitor, Gwen saw Markel already had the second man on his belly, handcuffing his wrists.

Gwen breathed, really breathed, for the first time in what felt like a long time.

Beside her, Rebecca said, "Well, that didn't go exactly as planned. At least Lacey is safe now, that's the important thing."

"There's that," Gwen groaned.

15

AFTERMATH

"THANK GOD IT'S OVER, APRIL," GWEN TOLD HER sister-in-law after they'd secured the scene.

Jake Bryant and the second poacher, identified by Ranger Paterson as Robert McConnell, were handcuffed and on their way to the county jail.

April and Gwen waited in Lacey's back yard watching the crime techs in the barn. The ambulance called to assist Lacey sat parked close by.

"I'm damned unhappy that the civilian we used was hurt, but the medics said she'd be fine, just bruised and shook up," April said. "Good news is we arrested a couple poachers, took down a drug supplier, and I bet after my detectives finish talking to Bryant and McConnell, we'll have solved a murder and laid a kidnapping and assault charge on them. Not bad for a night's work I'm thinking."

"Not bad at all," Gwen agreed.

Just then the back doors of the ambulance opened. One of the medics put his head out and asked them, "One of you Gwen Lindstrom?"

"That's me," Gwen replied, raising her hand.

"She'd like you to join us," he said, pointing inside where Lacey lay on a gurney.

"Go ahead," April told Gwen. To the medic, she asked, "You mind transporting them both to the hospital? I'm going to be busy here for a while, and our witness here—" she waved at hand toward Gwen— "will need a ride."

"No problem, Sheriff," he said and motioned Gwen to climb inside.

Lacey looked like hell. Her neck was red, swollen, and scratched where the rope had bound her. The purple ends of her dark tangled hair looked garish in the light of the ambulance's bay. The medics had covered her with a blanket, but her bruised eyes were wide and red-rimmed.

Gwen sat on the built-in bench and took one of Lacey's hands. She saw her nails were broken and dirty where Lacey had clawed at the rope.

"They said I'm going to be okay," she rasped. "Just going to take a while for my voice to come back and the swelling to go down."

Gwen worried that if she opened her mouth, she was going to cry, and that wouldn't do either of them any good. Instead, she nodded and gently squeezed her hand.

Lacey smiled and rasped, "I may need a couple days off, just until my voice goes back to normal."

The smile and Lacey's worry about her waitress job did start the tears. One of the medics handed Gwen a tissue and she wiped her eyes.

"Take whatever time you need," Gwen told Lacey. "The job will be waiting when you're ready to come back."

One of the medics went out the back door. Gwen heard the driver's door open and close. The motor started, red and blue lights flashed, and they were on the way to the hospital.

16

EPILOGUE

The case against Jake Bryant and Robert McConnell for Donald Myers' killing, Lacey's assault and kidnapping, and the drug manufacturing and poaching crimes would take a while to wind through the court system. Meanwhile, there were hungry customers to serve and a business for Gwen to run at the Ranchers' Café. Customers gossiped about events at the house hidden behind the trees. They asked Gwen about Lacey and her involvement, but she avoided commenting, saying it was still under investigation.

Lacey came back to work after a week of sick leave. By the end of the day, her voice grew hoarse again, but she was not the timid girl Gwen had hired. Instead, she walked with confidence and had lost most of the fidgety nervousness. Occasionally,

Gwen would even see her smile and laugh with one of the customers.

She'd also lost that gaunt waif look and put some meat on her skinny frame. Gwen gave Mack credit for that. He and Lacey had struck up a friendship after she came back to work. Lacey had stayed with Gwen for a while, but after Mack and his wife offered to rent the studio apartment above their garage to her, Lacey quickly accepted. The apartment came with a bonus; Mack gave her a standing invitation to have dinner with his family. In return, Lacey occasionally babysat for Mack's two grandchildren. It was an arrangement that suited all involved.

Best of all, the rangers, Todd and Mark, surprised Lacey by presenting her a check for five thousand dollars, the reward for information leading to the capture of the poachers.

Gwen reclaimed her house and the peace and quiet she'd come to enjoy.

If she got done early that day, she planned to spend the afternoon flitting one of her newly made flies across the surface of Wind River.

THE END

Dear reader,

We hope you enjoyed reading *POACH*. Please take a moment to leave a review, even if it's a short one. Your opinion is important to us.

Discover more books by Connie L. Beckett at https://www.nextchapter.pub/authors/connie-l-beckett

Want to know when one of our books is free or discounted? Join the newsletter at http://eepurl.com/bqqB3H

Best regards,
Connie L. Beckett and the Next Chapter Team

COMING SOON: MAZE, A GWEN LINDSTROM MYSTERY 2

Join Gwen in the second book of the mystery series as she investigates what happened to her late husband's pension money. It wasn't just Gabe's money that has gone missing, other long-time employees of Rhett Manufacturing have also lost their pensions. Efforts to find out what happened have failed. Seeking answers, Gwen is led through a maze of deception and into dangerous territory.

Want to read a Gwen Lindstrom short story mystery?

Visit the author's website at https://conniebeckett.net to sign up for Connie's newsletter, learn about upcoming books and events, and receive a free short story, *Ranchers' Café*. The restaurant Gwen Lindstrom owns is gossip central. After an ill-tempered local rancher is killed, Gwen keeps her ears open for clues that can help solve his murder.

POACH
ISBN: 978-4-86752-930-0
Large Print

Published by
Next Chapter
1-60-20 Minami-Otsuka
170-0005 Toshima-Ku, Tokyo
+818035793528

4th October 2021